Dark and Dangerous Things

M.A. Chiappetta

Donna A. Leahey

Margaret Perdue

L.A. Smith

The writers would like to thank

The members of Unbreakable Spines, Critical Ink, and South Tulsa Writers

Panera Bread, Barnes & Noble, and T.G.I. Fridays located on 41st street in Tulsa

The fine merchants of coffee, wine, and beer in Green Country, Oklahoma

And our friends and family who have given us the time to write.

Titus Luxor for creating the artwork

Also, the proofreading efforts of M.A. Chiappetta. Any mistakes remaining are due to our stubborn refusal to listen.

A special thank you to Donna A. Leahey, who braved the wilds of e-publishing to do the layout of our anthology.

TABLE OF CONTENTS

Under New Management

By M.A. Chiappetta

Officer Castro eyed me as he stirred another creamer into his paper coffee cup. I squirmed under his dark, probing gaze, hoping he wouldn't ask if I had skipped class again to hunt in the woods for the spaceship. Because I had. And I didn't want to lie.

No one believed me about the ship, but I knew what I'd seen—a silver streak across the sky, streaming trails of dark smoke like a dragon crashing to earth. The spherical UFO went down beneath the forest's canopy, where I couldn't see it anymore. Moments later, I heard a series of booms and then the ground shook. The rest of the town heard it too, felt the shaking. But no one else had seen the ship. They didn't believe me, not even when the alien walked into the diner's front door, asking for work in broken English.

He was short, squat, about four feet tall, with shuffling flat feet and exceptionally long fingers. His silvery, scaled face looked like it had been squashed in by a giant fist. Calling him ugly would have been generous. I couldn't understand why no one else was reacting. But as soon as I stuttered a confused question about his appearance, Mom pinched me and hissed in my ear, "Don't be rude! He's one of those short people, is all."

Everyone in the diner was staring at me like *I* was the weirdo. Even Jim looked disgusted. I didn't want to set my stepfather off, so I mumbled an apology and let him do the talking. He wanted someone to clean the bathrooms. The next thing I knew, poor Vergel, the silent crash survivor, was working in the diner as a lowly janitor. I was the only one who knew the truth.

(Well, my therapist knew. But when I told him, he asked if I ever hallucinated or heard voices. It was shaky at first. In the end we made a deal. I promised to work hard to "accept reality," and he promised not to prescribe me pills. I also decided privately not to think too much about why no one else could see what Vergel really was.)

I pulled my thoughts back to Castro, who was still studying me. The burly Italian officer didn't ask about the ship, the aliens, or even my therapist visits. He asked about the sign. "Michael, isn't it time to take that down?" He tilted his head toward the ragged paper hanging crookedly on the wall, scrawled with big red Sharpie letters:

Under New Management

"Jim says it brings in business," I muttered, "because customers like to help out a new guy." Which was stupid. Everyone in town knew we weren't new. But there was no arguing with Jim, who had a persistent delusion that this dumpy diner would make him rich one day.

"Speaking of Jim," Castro said carefully, "how's he been treating you and your Mom?"

I shrugged and traced the scratch marks worn into the weathered Formica countertop. What was there to say? The police came to our house every few months. Mom refused to press charges. Then the spaceship crashed, and I talked about it. Since then, Castro came in for coffee every day, asked about Jim and Mom, and sometimes about school. He thought I needed help and had a soft spot for kids with messed-up parents, like me. But I still didn't want to talk to him about my stepfather. The truth was too uncomfortable.

Jim drank too much. He got physical. Not so much toward me, mostly toward Mom. She was always arguing with him, especially when he drank. She threw things a lot. He shouted and slapped her a lot. Sometimes he threw things at me, but for some reason, he never slapped me. They both blamed their fighting on me, when half the time I wasn't even home when they'd started in on each other. Maybe it *was* my fault. I skipped school too much and came home too late at night.

But there was another reason I didn't want to talk bad about Jim. Weird as it was, Jim sometimes acted like he cared about me more than Mom did.

Like last fall, when he took me fishing. I'd never been fishing before, didn't know what to do, but Jim taught me how to cast a line. He didn't get drunk that day. When we came back to town, he offered to pay for a tattoo I'd been wanting, which was more than Mom had done for me lately.

I was halfway through the tattoo when Mom ran into the tattoo parlor screaming at us. As soon as the artist realized I wasn't eighteen, he stopped working on me, so that instead of a finished heart and the letters LIPPI—my last name—I only had half a heart and the letters LI. Mom definitely knew how to cause a scene. I rubbed my bicep, remembering it all.

Castro noticed. "You know," he teased, pointing at my arm, "you should finish that tattoo. Make it *library*. Since you love to study."

"Class valedictorian, that's me." I rolled my eyes, thinking of the classes I'd skipped, and wiped the counter to look busy because I didn't want to anger Jim.

"*Valedictorian*. Big word, Michael." Officer Castro laughed. "It's library for you all right. I heart libraries. Very macho."

"Shut up," I said. But I smiled. Castro was cool. Sometimes. He locked down the top of the coffee cup, then pulled a few bills out of his wallet and pushed them across the counter toward me. My eyes widened.

"That's yours," he said. "I'd pocket it fast if I were you."

I placed my cleaning rag over the bills, slid them off the counter, slipped them into my jeans. "Thanks," I whispered.

"If you ever need more money," he added, "or some help…ask me."

I nodded, my eyes focused on the counter as I rubbed a yellowed spot over and over, saying nothing. Castro sighed. I heard him leave, his footsteps a steady, confident thudding.

When the door jingled him out, I looked up, right into my stepfather's snakelike gaze. His scarred lips were pulled down into a mean grimace. "What was that about?" He hated Castro.

I froze, shoulders hunched, head down. "He was asking me about school. Made fun of my tattoo."

Jim stared at me. I didn't move. Finally, he shook his head in contempt. "If you were a man, you'd go back to the tattoo parlor and get that damned thing finished. Fuck your mother."

Easy for you to say, I thought. But I swallowed the words and said instead, "I don't have the money for it."

A harsh, long laugh rumbled out of my stepfather's mouth. "Officer Castro didn't give you enough?"

I sucked in a sharp breath. "He didn't give me any

money," I lied. My stepfather smirked, then slapped his hand on the counter. I flinched, wanting to disappear. He had me trapped.

But then the alien came to my rescue. I called him Vergel because that was as close as I could come to saying his actual name. "Lunch?" he asked, poking my pocket with what I assumed was his thumb.

"It's too damn early for lunch," Jim snapped. "Get back to work! The floor needs mopping."

The little creature cocked his head left and right, like he always did when he pretended not to understand something. Then he repeated, more insistently: "Lunch!" He poked my pocket again. This time I got the message.

"Oh, lunch! Yeah, that's— That's what Officer Castro said. Wanted to treat us to lunch. That's what the money is for."

I waited, listening to the clattering of pots as Mom cooked in the kitchen. For a few moments, I thought Vergel and I might get away with it. Then Jim stuck out his hand, palm up. "Let me see what kind of lunch you're having."

Swallowing my frustration, I yanked the cash out and surrendered it. He fingered through the bills—ten, twenty, thirty. "Lot of cash for lunch." He plucked two bills for himself and gave me the remaining one. "I'll just save this in your college account, eh?" He laughed as he slapped the kitchen door open and vanished behind it.

I sighed down at the ten dollar bill. "Guess it's burgers again, Vergel." I swore the squat, silver creature sighed back before he shuffled away to grab the mop. I watched him in wonder; I didn't know aliens could sigh.

Later, Vergel and I climbed a scrubby, sunburned grass hill by the forest edge and sat in the humid shade of a giant oak. The little alien appeared to be frowning, though I wasn't sure. It was hard to decipher his facial expressions; his face was so different than mine. His lips split vertically as well as horizontally, like those paper fortune tellers the girls used in elementary school when they tried to get me to kiss them. Vergel's eyes were as wide as my palm, round and silver-black, and they didn't blink. Once, though, I caught him nodding off, and it looked like thin, iridescent skins had clicked down over his eyes. Like a lizard. It was cool in a weird way. I still couldn't believe no one else could see his real face.

I was glad to split a fast-food meal with him. It got us away from the diner. I handed him some fries, which he placed carefully on a napkin in front of his knees. He always ate kneeling. When I handed him his burger, he pulled up the broken, ketchup-sogged bun and made a tiny irked sound.

"Sorry, it's all they had for ten dollars, Vergel."

The little alien patted my shoulder, as though to reassure me. "Lunch," he said.

"Yeah." I bit into my own burger—and then remembered something. "Oh, yeah," I mumbled, still chewing. I took a sip of my cola, then reached with one hand into the fast food bag, still holding the burger in my other hand. When my fingers hit the chilled plastic container, I grinned.

"Surprise!" I gave Vergel a package of carrot salad, complete with parsley and raisins. Gross, if you asked me. But Vergel's eyes sparkled, and he oohed softly.

"Lunch?" He sounded happy. My grin widened.

"Yeah! They're trying this new vegetarian menu. It was kind of expensive, but Marnie gave me a free sample." I passed Vergel a spoon. He eagerly opened up the package, humming a little tune that he often hummed while he cleaned. I called it "Party among the Stars" because I liked to think it was a song with a name. A happy name.

"Mmm!" Vergel made tiny sounds of delight as he ate. I lay back on the grass, the ground soft and warm like a blanket underneath me. I felt expansively relaxed.

"What's up there anyway?" I wondered, my eyes fixed on the clouds above.

Vergel pointed to the western sky. "Home," he mused.

I cocked my head toward him, curious. "Do you ever feel alone?"

Vergel's eyes turned toward the oak above us, and he hummed a new tune, bittersweet. He shook his hands above his chest. His sign for *no*. He tapped my hand, just once, and quietly said, "Good friend Michael."

His words caught me by surprise. I'd never had many friends. Embarrassed, I rubbed a tear away and fixed my gaze on the sky, the breeze stirring my hair, the earth holding me up.

"Yes," I agreed, my voice rough with an emotion I didn't want to name. "Friends."

The afternoon lull turned into a dinner rush, and by the time we closed up for the night, the diner was a mess. Dirty dishes were piled everywhere. Vergel was mopping up the bathroom because the toilet had overflowed. A group of college kids skipped out on their tab, which infuriated my stepfather. Now Jim was in a shouting match with Mom in the kitchen. I didn't like it. They hardly ever fought in the diner. Something was off tonight. It made me jumpy.

"I'm not kidding, Jeanine!" Jim yelled. "How many

times do I have to tell you to keep an eye on those goddamned kids?"

Mom was banging pots and pans in the sink while she yelled back. "I was keeping an eye on them, you ass!" I winced at her harsh tone.

Helpless and edgy, I kept bussing tables because I didn't know what else to do. Experience had taught me that interfering just made things worse. My hands were trembling. I nearly dropped a handful of silverware. But I caught everything before it crashed to the floor. Relieved not to have attracted attention, I sucked in a deep breath and counted like my therapist told me to do when I felt like I was floating away. It wasn't helping. I felt sick.

Jim kept screaming, his words hitting the air so hard that I flinched. "The hell you were! You were eyeing that prissy lawyer you dated in high school! You're sleeping with him, aren't you?"

A loud slamming noise followed Jim's accusation, as if he was pounding the kitchen counter with his fists. My mother laughed—a bitter, mocking noise that grated on me. I stared at the kitchen door, the silverware forgotten.

"Well, you can't blame me," she sneered. "That's right, you heard me." She laughed louder. "At least that man has the decency to shave and keep fit and treat me like a woman!"

I couldn't believe what I was hearing. My hands gripped the bussing tub so hard, my fingertips went numb. The diner sank into an uneasy hush. All I could hear was my own heart pounding in my ears.

One…two…three…don't forget to breathe…it's okay to breathe, to keep breathing…

Jim spoke very softly. I couldn't make out the words, but I didn't have to. He never got that quiet unless he was about to do something vicious. I moved toward the kitchen, my chest heaving. As I placed my trembling hand on the kitchen door, I heard a thunderous crash. Then a tiny, feminine moan. Then nothing.

Shaking, I pushed the door inward, my feet moving without thought. The room felt static, like lightning had just struck. Jim loomed over the sink, his eyes stormy. His face was redder than I'd ever seen it, almost purple. His hands hung by his side, fingers curled. I stared at him for I don't know how long.

Then I saw my mother.

She lay on the floor by the oven, curled on her side as though sleeping, one arm stretched over her head, the other bent across her abdomen. Her legs were splayed wide. The back of her head was gashed and bleeding so heavily that a pool was forming on the scuffed-up tiles. Her soft brown hair floated in the bloody puddle. I don't know how long I stood there before the numb fog lifted and I realized what I was seeing.

My mother… Jim had just…

No.

"Mom?" I stumbled toward her, my voice ragged. "Mommy, it's me, it's Michael." Jim grabbed my shoulder, his voice much too calm.

"Leave her."

I blinked at him, unable to make sense of what he was saying. Maybe he had called the police already. Shaking him off, I staggered forward and fell to my knees by my mother's head. My quivering hands hovered above her face. "Mom?" I whispered. Slowly, trembling, I pushed away the thin curls that had fallen over her eyes. My fingers traced her neck, feeling for a heartbeat. A heartbeat that wasn't there.

"Oh God," I rasped, my breaths shallow and painful. "Oh God."

Jim tugged at me. "Get up!" he hissed. I hadn't even heard him come over, but there he was, glaring at me. I looked up at him, confused. When I didn't move, he slapped me hard, and yanked me to my feet. "I said get up!"

"But Mom…" I swallowed the bile rising up in my throat as I glanced at her too-still body, crumpled on the floor.

Jim's fist squeezed my arm until I gasped in pain. "Your mother had it coming," he hissed. "She came at me with a knife. You were here. You saw it."

I shook my head, not realizing what Jim was implying. "No, I didn't see that."

Jim's eyes grew dark with rage. "Oh yes you did. You saw everything just like I said." He shoved me backward against the counter. The cold metal edge stabbed into my lower back, the sudden startling pain making me gasp. Fear rushed through me. I tried to push Jim away. But he was stronger than me. He twisted my arm until I thought it would break.

"Jim," I begged. "Please! She's my mom!" She lay so still. Like stone. "Please! Let me call the ambulance. I won't tell anyone what happened. I'll say she tripped."

"There will be no ambulances." Jim's voice was soft, dark, void of emotion. "Get me?"

"No problem," I blurted, thinking I could placate him. "I can take her to the hospital myself. She tripped, but she'll be okay. Right?"

Jim's fist closed over my throat, choking me to silence. My eyes widened in shock. When he placed the butcher knife's icy blade against my cheek, I went limp. He was going to kill me. Kill me like he had just killed…

"No hospitals," he warned.

I stifled a frightened moan as the laser-sharp knife traced a thin, painful line down my face. Afraid to move, I tried to say *no hospitals*, but couldn't get the words out.

"Nothing happened here," Jim told me. "You get me? Your mother had it coming. You won't say or do anything." The blade slid down to my Adam's apple. Something felt hot and wet against my skin. He'd cut me, drawn blood. I couldn't move. "You tell your Officer Castro," Jim warned, "and I will kill him and make you watch."

"I…won't…tell…" The words scraped their way out of my throat.

"And your doctor. Don't even think about telling him anything."

"I—I won't."

Jim's hand moved around to the back of my neck, and he pressed me close to him, so close I could smell the scotch on his breath. My eyes met his. "Not a word," he insisted softly, "or I'll cut you into little pieces until you bleed to death."

"Not a word," I repeated obediently, shaking so hard that I feared I'd pee myself any second. Jim loosed the scruff of my neck, shoving me into the counter. As I caught myself to keep from falling, I noticed a grey silhouette reflected in the metallic toaster that my mother had insisted on putting near the stove.

Vergel. He'd seen and heard everything. My head turned toward him. *Run*, I mouthed. But Vergel remained there watching me, watching Jim. He glanced, just once, at my mother. Then he sighed.

"Vergel clean spill?" he asked.

I stared at him. Was it possible he didn't know what he was seeing? Was it possible he didn't know my mother was dead? Or did he think it didn't matter? "What…what do you mean?" I asked. "I don't understand."

"He means he'll help me, won't you, Vergel?" Jim studied me, eyes half-lidded, snakelike. "Like you should be doing, Michael. Helping me clean up this…spill."

"Vergel help," the alien chirped, as though all was normal. What kind of friend did that?

Suddenly, I heard myself screaming. "She's not a spill, Vergel, she's my *mother*!"

The little alien looked at me, sadness in his expression. "Vergel clean spill," he insisted, shuffling up to Jim with the mop. Something in me snapped. I rushed forward and shoved Vergel into the wall, shouting wordlessly. Then I slammed open the kitchen door and fled through the dining area, out the front door, unable to see where I was going through the tears in my eyes. Jim shouted after me, warning me to keep quiet, but who was I going to tell? Not Officer Castro. I didn't want Jim to kill him. Or my therapist either. And Vergel had abandoned me when I needed him most.

Grief-stricken, I ran until I couldn't run anymore. My legs spasmed in hot agony. As I blindly grasped for support, my hand splayed against the rough bark of a tree. I'd run straight into the forest and hadn't even realized it. Leaning against the tree trunk, I panted for breath, my chest aching. The area didn't look familiar. I didn't know where I was.

My mother was dead. Jim wanted to kill me. Vergel had turned his back on me and offered to help Jim. And now I was lost.

I slid to the ground and cried.

I awoke in the middle of the night to a strange singing sound, like jingling glass bells. Rubbing sleep from my eyes, I sat up on the forest floor, where I must have passed out after all my tears. I felt cold, achy, and confused.

Until the memories flooded in. Jim…the diner…my mother…the blood… Vergel…

No. I didn't want to remember. I wanted to sleep and forget. But I wasn't sure I was safe. I creaked to my feet, wondering where to go, and saw something moving among the trees. A tiny, fuzzy blue-green light swayed waist-height above the forest floor, several feet from where I stood. It moved slowly toward me, then slowly away, then hovered waiting, a hypnotic sight to my tired mind. Half-asleep, I followed it along a dark forest path, fallen leaves making a hushed rustling under my feet. Several minutes passed before it occurred to me that I didn't know what the blue-green light was, or why I was following it.

I stopped, hesitant, my thoughts like molasses.

"Mom?" I asked, wondering if she had come to save me. But she couldn't have. She was dead. Hot tears formed at the corners of my eyes, blurring my vision. I started shaking.

The blue-green light hovered in place. Then a gaggle of bright voices rose up. Shadows emerged from the woods—small, stout figures with skin of grey, blue, green, and purple. They enveloped me, six or seven of them, gazing up at me with their enormous eyes, touching my arms and hands with their long, silvery fingers.

A cry caught in my throat. I slipped to my knees, covering my head, rocking back and forth. "This is not happening," I moaned between choked sobs. "I can't—" I hiccupped. "—can't do this."

A hand I recognized touched my chin, pushed my head

up. I looked straight into Vergel's eyes. He looked so sad.

"You! You helped Jim," I cried as I tried without success to push him away. My whole body hurt as if I'd been sick for days. "How could you do that to me?"

"Vergel not help Jim," the little alien said, his voice calming, his hands soothing as they petted my hair. "Vergel save Michael."

The other aliens, Vergel's kin, repeated his words, the different timbres of their voices making my name sound musical. They drew closer, patting my shoulders and squeezing my hands. It was strange…but comforting. My shuddering sobs eased up. Soon, I knelt in near silence, sucking in deep breaths, exhausted.

"Come," Vergel said, gently prodding me to my feet. The brush rustled, and one more alien emerged from the bushes, the blue-green light turning out to be a strange, alien lantern in his hands, curved like a rising flame. It was so beautiful that I wanted to cry, and I realized I was close to falling apart again.

The lantern-bearing alien looked at Vergel. "Home?" he asked. My friend nodded. He took my hand in his and drew me forward, the other aliens crowded around me like a pack of protective puppies. I was so numb I didn't even ask where we were going. Soon we arrived at a wide clearing. In the center, glowing a rich green, was a large sphere with antennae and pipes, and I couldn't guess what else running along its outer casing.

"Holy crap," I whispered, awed by the thing's alien beauty.

Vergel made a soft puffing sound. Laughter. He patted me on the back, still laughing. "Welcome home, Michael."

Propelled by Vergel's firm hand, I walked halfway up

the entrance ramp before an important question made me pause. "What about Jim?" I asked. "And…and Mom?"

Vergel urged me into the ship. "Michael sleep now. Everything else later." He whistled his tune again. "Vergel smart, you know."

I nodded slowly. "Yeah, I believe it." I stumbled tiredly into the spaceship that no one believed existed, where I could be safe from everything, including Jim.

I woke up thirsty. My eyes followed the steel grey walls that curved up to a gentle arching point above me, then took in the aquamarine light in which I floated. It looked like water, and it rippled in time with my breaths.

Where? Oh yeah, the spaceship.

Drowsy, I sank back down into bedding so soft it could have been a cloud, and shut my eyes, falling slowly down into sleep again. I'd get water later. But an alien finger poked my chest. I stirred and found Vergel looking down at me.

"Up," he urged.

"No," I complained, groggy. "I'm tired." But the smell of blood and Jim's alcohol flooded my mind. I swallowed bile. "Oh, God, Vergel, what am I going to do?" He tilted his head side to side, as though confused.

"Go to work," he said. My stomach twisted.

"Are you crazy? I can't go there!"

"Michael. Yes—"

I balled myself up in the farthest corner of the bed. "No, I can't! Jim will kill me, he'll kill us all!"

Vergel reached for me, as though to pull me out of the floating cloud bed. Panicked, I struggled to push him away, but he was too strong. He was tugging me out of bed, away from safety. My breathing grew ragged, chest tight, throat closing up. I tried to scream but couldn't get enough air. I was hyperventilating.

Around me, the sea-colored lights pulsed faster and faster. Alien voices chattered, Vergel's voice distinct among them, but I couldn't understand their words. Alarming wheezing noises burst past my lips. The more I struggled to inhale, the harder it got to breathe. My fingers curled into my left thigh, the pain faint and far away as my vision dimmed.

A tight glasslike mask came down over my nose and mouth. Moaning in protest, I tried to tug it off. But the aliens held me down until soothing warmth filled my limbs, making me sleepy. Flickering images flashed across the metal walls, glimpses of the diner, my mother, me—moving so fast I couldn't make sense of what I was seeing. And I didn't want to. My toes tingled pleasantly. I sank into the bedding, my breath easing as oxygen filled my lungs.

I floated like that for a while, in twilight. When I finally stirred, Vergel pushed sweaty hair off my forehead with an alien expression that mirrored the frown Officer Castro gave me when I behaved badly in his presence. Thinking of Castro reminded me of Jim's threats. If I wasn't careful, I'd get all the people who cared about me killed. All three of them. Mom made four, but… I turned my head toward the wall and swallowed my tears, refusing to cry.

The aliens chattered amongst themselves, but Vergel spoke English, so I could follow the conversation. They were trying to decide what to do with me.

"Diner," Vergel insisted. It sounded like some of the others disagreed. I watched them, feeling scared and numb and deep down somewhere, very angry, as they argued.

"No kill Michael," one said clearly, the one who had held the lantern the night before when they found me.

Vergel shook his hands *no*. "Protect Michael!"

A heated discussion broke out that I couldn't follow. I pulled the alien oxygen mask off my face and cut through their argument with my own voice, loud and clear.

"If I go back, Jim will kill me. He will kill Vergel, and Officer Castro, and my therapist, and I refuse to be responsible for that." Never mind that I was responsible for my mother's death by not walking into the kitchen sooner and taking her place. But that was a thought for another time, so I pushed it aside and sat up, my muscles taut with the urge to hit something.

"No one dies anymore," I announced, my voice hard with anger. "Nobody else dies."

The aliens stood quietly. The only sound was my harsh, ugly, human breathing. But I didn't waver. Abruptly, Vergel huffed his little laugh. He was laughing at me! My body flushed hot, and I tightened my fist, but he patted my hand gently.

"Not even Jim?" he asked. Around him, the aliens visibly startled. Then they began whispering. A couple of them prodded Vergel's arms to get his attention. He waved his hands *no* and pointed to me. "Michael?" he asked.

I knew what he was asking. I shook my head, not wanting to answer. But it was clear that Vergel, alien though he was, had put me on a human hook of morality and was waiting to see what I would do about it.

"Jim is going to kill people," I said, staring into Vergel's demanding silver eyes. Then I sighed. "I don't think I can kill him though. That's not me."

Vergel whistled a short, happy tune. "Yes. No killing." His lips twisted into an excellent imitation of a human smile. "Michael—" He added a word I didn't recognize, something from his own language. All the aliens patted me with gentle, soothing touches, humming along with Vergel, repeating the magical word and nodding. I'd never seen Vergel nod, not even once. But now all the aliens were doing it and smiling at me too. I must have passed a test.

"What are you saying?" I asked. Vergel paused, tilted his head as he mused, then nodded again. "Michael… *Man*."

"Man?" I was confused. "Yeah, I'm a man, but…"

Vergel's hands waved again. "Not human. *Man*. Strong. Brave. Better than Jim."

My mouth opened in a silent *oh*. I chewed my lip. "But I'm hiding!" I blurted. "I'm scared of Jim." I thought of my mother, how I hadn't wanted to risk going into the kitchen the night before. "I've always been scared of Jim," I admitted.

The little alien held his hands wide, looking so human in that moment. "So? Diner." He tugged at me, and this time I allowed him to get me to my feet.

"What are we going to do when we get back to the diner?" I asked.

Vergel huffed a short, dangerous laugh. "Help Jim," he suggested with what I swore was a decidedly human touch of sarcasm. For the first time since I'd met him, I wondered if the little alien was less passive than I'd imagined. A shiver ran up my spine.

We hiked through the woods, Vergel and his friends and me. I tried to talk with them, but other than insisting that we go to the diner, I didn't know what they planned to do. Too quickly for comfort, we arrived in town. A bitter taste rose in my mouth as I looked at the diner's cloudy windows, the dirty sidewalk, the cheap name sign that swung at an unreadable angle because only one side of it was hooked properly to the roof; the other side hung loose. One day that sign was going to come crashing down. That's what Mom had always said, but Jim would never fix the damned thing.

My hands curled into tight fists. Trembling with the fire that raged through me, I stepped across the doorstep. But then I froze in foggy surprise.

I couldn't believe what I was seeing. The diner was open for business! Only a few guys were there, much smaller than our usual morning crowd. But still. They sat there eating eggs and toast. Like everything was fine.

Suddenly, the scent of bleach hit me, mixed with bacon grease. Gagging, I turned to run. But Vergel blocked me. His friends crowded around the door, all watching me. Vergel insisted, "No fear, Michael. Time to eat."

After a moment, I nodded. I wouldn't eat, but Vergel was right about going inside. I didn't want to run anymore. It was time to confront Jim. I walked toward the kitchen, nervous but determined. As I reached the counter, Jim slammed through the kitchen door, a plate of eggs and bacon in his hand. He halted when he saw me.

"So," he growled. "You're back."

My throat tightened. Remembering his hands choking me, the knife pressed against my face, I stepped back, smack into Vergel. My alien friend pushed me gently forward.

"Meet friends," he announced to everyone, pointing to the aliens that crowded in the doorway, their voices chattering and their heads whipping around in amazement at all the humans. "Here for breakfast!"

"What the...?" Jim swallowed hard, his Adam's apple bouncing tightly up and down. "What the hell is this, Michael?" He glared at me, as though I had brought home a gaggle of gang members, not these calm, peaceful creatures. Briefly, I wondered what he saw when he looked at them. Did they seem human to him, as Vergel apparently did?

Vergel nudged my leg, tugging my thoughts away from unneeded questions. Mysteries could wait. Time to be brave.

They're my friends, Jim." I pushed the words past my clenched teeth. "They want breakfast."

"Breakfast," the aliens echoed. Their musical voices and their support sent warmth through my veins. I stood up straighter and met Jim's gaze squarely.

"You won't mind if I seat them. They have money." I knew my stepfather. The man couldn't turn down a dollar if it bit him and drew blood. He narrowed his eyes, his features scrunched in distrust, but I looked him in the eye until a trace of doubt flickered across his face. Another rush of strength flooded me as I realized I had, in fact, successfully lied to Jim. And he couldn't do anything about it.

"Show me the money," he said, voicing his doubt. But his eyes flicked to and fro, watching the aliens with what seemed like nervousness. *Of course!* I thought with a surge of confidence. *He's afraid because there are a lot of them. And they're with me!*

Vergel held out a wad of cash to Jim, surprising everyone, including me. One of the customers whistled appreciatively. Jim shot the man an annoyed glance. Then he snatched the money, pocketed it, and nodded to the far corner of the diner, which was currently empty. "Seat 'em over there, away from my *preferred* customers," he ordered.

The aliens needed no further urging. Quickly, they

settled at the empty tables, some sitting with webbed feet dangling, the rest standing, their long fingers resting on the tabletops. They all watched me.

"Get plates," Vergel urged, waving me toward the kitchen. I balked, thinking of my Mom lying on the floor.

"I don't want to go in there," I told him.

"Trust Vergel, Michael."

As I hesitated, I caught Jim studying me. "Is there a problem, Michael?"

I heard the sharp edge of warning in his voice and thought of Officer Castro and my therapist. The danger they'd be in. Reluctantly, I shook my head.

"Then serve your *friends*," Jim snapped. He set the plate down and sat, apparently planning to eat breakfast while I worked. "We haven't got all day. There's a lot to do around here. Things to clean up."

Rage tightened my fists. I stepped toward Jim, but Vergel gripped my forearm and pulled me into the kitchen. The counter was covered in broken eggs. Jim couldn't cook to save his life. Mom had always done that. I looked for her. But she was gone, the floor clean.

Hot tears in my eyes, I whirled on Vergel. "What am I supposed to do now? You heard him. He's going to kill us! That's what he has to clean up! You and me!"

Instead of answering, Vergel approached the stove, where a large pot rested, steam arising from whatever it held. That was weird. We never served stew, or chili, or anything like that. Whatever Jim was cooking smelled foul. I put a hand on the pot's lid to look inside. But the small alien tugged me away.

"No," he insisted.

The set of Vergel's face and his tone of voice made me shiver. My gaze drifted back toward the stove, as if my eyes had a will of their own. A horrible thought occurred to me. "Jim wouldn't have… I mean, even he couldn't have…" But really, what wouldn't Jim do if he could commit murder? My throat burned. Suddenly I was vomiting into a corner of the kitchen, my head replaying what Vergel had said last night. *Vergel clean spill.*

"You didn't, did you?" I begged, wiping my mouth with my sleeve. "Please, please tell me you didn't." Unable to say the words, I pointed a shaking finger at the pot.

Vergel waddled over and took my hand. "Never! Vergel protect Michael. Michael run. Jim send Vergel to clean bathroom. Vergel not see what Jim do." The little alien glanced at the pot on the stove and sighed. "Vergel not surprised."

It was the most he had ever said at one time. I stared at him, not sure whether to cry or hug him. I needed to throw up again. My guts were on fire. I had to get out of the kitchen. Just then, the outer door jingled as someone came in. I peered out of the kitchen. Officer Castro stood at the counter, his expression clouded with suspicion as he watched Jim shovel eggs into his mouth.

Fear smothered the last bits of my courage. "Oh, God, he's going to kill all three of us, right now!"

"Be strong, Michael." The alien prodded me through the kitchen door. Jim stared at me, his eyes poisonous. I stared back, disgusted that I ever wanted him to like me. I hated him so much. And I was right to hate him. He deserved it.

Officer Castro disrupted my thoughts. "Michael. You all right?"

"Am I all right?" My voice sounded tight and funny,

even to me. Jim straightened, his palms pressed into the table as he watched me. Castro flicked his gaze toward Jim, then back to me.

"Michael, you don't look right. You're pale." Castro studied me a moment. "That's vomit on your shirt. Are you sick?" His eyes pierced me, like he knew the truth. I wanted to tell him. But if I did, Jim might hurt someone.

"It's okay," I lied. "I'm fine."

"The hell you are," Castro growled. "Talk to me."

Jim laughed suddenly, startling the whole diner. Everyone turned to him. "No one wants to hear the kid bitch," he said.

Castro shifted in his seat as though ready for trouble. But his voice was so calm, I thought maybe I imagined it. "I don't mind hearing anything Michael has to say," he told Jim.

My stepfather laughed again. "Kid's been out all night. Haven't you, Michael?" He spoke my name like a warning. "Who the hell knows what you've been up to? Your *mother* and I have been so worried."

Something snapped in me then. "Don't talk about my mother!" I shouted. It was as though my fear had been swept away by an ocean of red. Vergel's hand tugged at my back, a reminder that he was there. I wasn't alone.

"I'll handle this," I hissed. "Move back." The alien blew out his breath softly. Then he nodded and slipped into the kitchen. I didn't know what he was doing but I didn't care. All I cared about was making my stepfather tell the truth.

"Michael, what's going on?" Castro demanded.

Before I could speak, Jim jumped in, the warning clear in the hard set of his shoulders and arms. "You're the one who shouldn't talk. Do I need to remind you what we agreed on?"

I stood there shaking, furious, determined to make Jim tell the truth, even if it killed me. No one else was going to die because of me. Mom was enough. I slid my hand along the counter, until my fingers hit upon a butter knife. I held it close to my waist, ready to fight.

Officer Castro studied me. Then he flicked loose the retention strap on his holster and faced Jim. The human customers watched open-mouthed, but no one said a word. The aliens huddled together, looking unafraid. I admired that. Jim terrified me. A sudden wave of nausea hit me. I gagged, then rested a hand on the counter to steady myself. Castro flicked his eyes toward me, so fast, then back to my stepfather.

"Jim," he said, voice deceptively calm. "Where's Jeanine?"

My stepfather's shoulders hunched, but his tone was defiant. "I told you. Michael ran off. She went to look for him. God knows where she is."

"He's not the only one," I whispered.

"Michael?" Castro prompted. "Talk to me."

"Last night…" I heard rustling, saw my stepfather moving cautiously in his seat, and wondered what he was up to. "Jim is right," I said in a rush. "I ran away. That part is true."

Castro's eyes flashed like fire. He was not a man I wanted to turn against me. "What's the part you haven't told me?"

Mom, I mouthed. Tears threatened again. I rubbed them away, my hand trembling.

"His mother ran off," Jim said. "The bitch left the kid. I

don't suppose you'll find her. Bet she just disappeared." He started to laugh.

"You lying bastard!" I screamed, tears rolling down my cheeks. "I wish you were dead!"

"Michael!" Castro sounded appalled. In that moment of distraction, Jim jerked to his feet, a gun in his hand. The officer yanked his weapon free. Aimed. Jim was pulling the trigger. He was going to beat Castro to the shot.

Suddenly, Jim's arm jerked up. The gun flew from his hand and cracked loudly against the wall. Clattered to the floor. Human customers shouting. Aliens rising up in the most enraged song I had ever heard. Every single one of them pointed at Jim, their eyes glowing cobalt. My stepfather stood engulfed in an aura of blue. He struggled in vain to escape. The blue mist that surrounded him flooded his nostrils, ears, mouth, until his eyes rolled up in his head. He collapsed, convulsing and grunting in obvious pain.

He deserved that pain. But I still felt sick.

Castro came up out of the crouch he'd instinctively dropped into when Jim pulled the gun. The officer's eyes roved over the entire diner before coming to rest on me. "Michael, explain this."

"Explain?" A frayed chuckle burst from my lips. "Well, there's a lot more aliens than I thought."

"Damn it, Michael," he snapped. "Explain. Now!"

I felt another panic attack coming on. Before it hit, I forced words past my tightening chest. "My mom…" My throat closed up. I couldn't say it.

Just then, Vergel stepped out of the kitchen, something small cradled in his hands. The little alien cocked his head at Jim's twitching body, then stepped up to the counter and stood on his tiptoes to set down a bowl in front of Castro. He pushed me away before I could see much, but I saw enough.

A finger with a torn-off nail.

"Mom," I whispered.

Vergel placed his long fingers against my forearm. The tightness in my chest eased, my head cleared. Startled, I met his silver gaze. Had he just stopped my panic attack? Before I could ask, he nudged the officer.

"Evidence against Jim," Vergel announced. He gestured toward his friends, who still held Jim captive in the blue aura. "Michael with us. Alibi. Witnesses."

Castro winced at the sight of the finger. He glanced at me. At last, I found my voice again.

"Jim killed my mother last night," I said. It felt like a confession of my own guilt. "My mom is dead because he killed her." Then I turned and vomited into the garbage pail behind the counter, the taste hot and bitter on my tongue.

Things changed a lot in a year.

The diner, sparkling clean and bright with a new paint job, bustled with good energy. Aliens filled the seats, chatting in the languages of the stars as they ate and shared stories of their lives with our human customers who, after a bit of shock, adapted to their presence and welcomed them into our community with open arms.

Vergel turned out to be an excellent cook. And I was better at math and business than I'd realized. We'd made the diner a success. It was something out of a movie—a story with a happy ending. I'd never seen a happy ending before in real life. But I liked it.

I set down an order of eggs in front of a human customer, followed by a plate of vegetables and fresh grass in front of one of the aliens. Then I strolled over to Officer Castro, who was adjusting the creamer in his coffee cup.

"Sure we can't get you anything else?" I asked. "It's on the house."

Castro shook his head. "I can't take food on the house. It's against the law." He studied me. "Why don't you call me Frank?"

"Your first name?" I asked. "Really?"

"You're a man now, Michael. So, yeah, call me Frank."

"Okay," I said. "Frank." I grinned ear to ear, unable to keep my delight hidden. It felt good to be a man. To be recognized for it.

Castro—*Frank*—laughed. Then his eyes locked on my shoulder. My hand slid up to cover the tattoo. Too late. Frank raised an eyebrow. "You got that thing finished?"

"I got it done out of town," I said, thinking of Mark, the tattoo artist who had snuck me into his shop a few nights ago, talking the entire time about how illegal the whole thing was because I was only seventeen, and how I shouldn't have asked him to help me—which I hadn't—and then admitting he was just trying to show me some respect for what I'd gone through.

Frank wasn't fooled. "Give me a break, and show me what Mark did for you." When I hesitated, he added, "I'm not on duty right now. I can…well…hear things without *hearing* them, if you know what I mean."

I shifted my arm to show off the entire tattoo. In my mind's eye, I could picture what Frank was seeing—the heart neatly completed, the red shading, the blue and green ribbon, the bold black lettering finished in the way that made the most sense, given everything that had happened.

"Libre," the officer read, his voice quiet. "Free." He looked at me. "Mark does nice work. And this fits better than library," he added, a grin playing over his lips.

"A little bit," I agreed, my smile matching his.

Just then, Vergel wandered over, carrying a cheese Danish wrapped in a small brown bag. He passed it to Frank with his mouth wide in what I now knew was the little alien's version of a smile. Then he patted me on the arm and said, "Lunch?"

"Isn't it too early for lunch?" Frank asked. A brief taste of sadness rose up in me, a reminder of things past, an opportunity to protect someone that I had lost because I didn't act in time. But the bubbling noise of happy humans and aliens filled the café—*my* café, *my* future, a happy place—and I couldn't help but feel my heart lighten.

"No way," I said, grateful to have two good friends—one a small silvery creature, the other a burly Italian cop—to share the here-and-now with. My therapist would have been proud to see me. And so would Mom.

"Vergel's right." I smiled into the moment. "Let's have lunch."

The Moon Dial

By Margaret Perdue

It was well past midnight and Steven still had not made a decision. His eyes scanned the ballroom yet again, resting for a moment here or there on some pretty young thing, but no one really struck his fancy. When he let out a bored sigh, his best friend Bernard responded to his malaise.

"The night's not getting any younger, Steven. You might as well resign yourself to taking the easiest and get it over with. Don't want to get stuck out at daybreak and have to spend your rest in a blasted, filthy tunnel again."

Steven knew his friend was right. His recent boredom with hunting had made him take unnecessary risks lately. Once it even resulted in his having to spend the entire day in a sewer drain before he could resurface, making it back to the rooms he shared with Bernard stinking like a wet rat.

It was so easy for Bernard! Not only was the other man recently transformed, which meant the thrill of the hunt was unparalleled excitement for him, but he preferred the company of men. And since men in London in 1811 had more freedom of movement than women, Bernard's work was much easier. All he had to do was find an interested party, and off they went to a club or kept rooms where privacy would not be an issue.

Steven, however, never had developed a taste for masculinity and preferred females, but they were so complicated! They flirted with him shamelessly, then refused to get into his carriage or insisted they invite their chaperone. Not that he didn't have his fill of successes; he did. Bored wives or adventurous debutantes or willing servant girls, he had enjoyed them all. Still, his reputation was beginning to blacken, as it always did after a time. Soon it would be necessary for him to move on again, as gruesome gossip had already started to surround him.

Gazing around again at the ladies in the room, Steven heard a voice behind him that set his teeth on edge.

"What ho, there, McElroy! I'd like a word with you."

"God's teeth!" Steven clenched his hand around his wineglass. "It's that blasted dimwit, Charles Wooldridge, again."

"Yes," said Bernard snidely. "And he's headed this way."

Charles Wooldridge was a personage Steven did not want to deal with tonight. He and his wife, Clarissa, had recently invited Steven to stay at their country house as part of a shooting party. Steven shouldn't have gone; it was far too dangerous, as Bernard had pointed out. Too many questions might be asked about Steven keeping odd hours and only eating the smallest bit of food and all. But the crushing boredom of his life had made Steven bold. And, of course, Bernard had been right.

"See here, McElroy… I need to ask you some rather pointed questions concerning your stay at my home recently." Wooldridge tried to puff himself up to appear larger in height than in girth to Steven. He was accompanied by two other fat, middle-aged aristocrats who were also trying to look intimidating.

"Wooldridge!" Steven turned on his charm and patted

the man on the shoulder. "How good to see you! What the devil is all this about?"

Caught off guard by the younger man's friendliness, Charles was unsure how to proceed.

"Well, it's…um…it's about the maids. They…um…well…they all got sick, you see… And Clarissa too! The doctor's been 'round, and he said it seems as if they look…well…very tired, like their health's been drained. Clarissa couldn't even come tonight; doctor said she had to stay in bed. Put up a damned fuss about it too!"

"I'll just bet she did, knowing I was to be here," thought Steven. Bernard gave him a knowing wink.

"Just how is all this my fault, Charles?"

The little fat man faltered again. "Oh, not saying it is. Not at all, but it does make one wonder. You see, the same thing seems to have happened when you stayed with Bertram here." He pointed to one of the men standing behind him. Bertram coughed and tried to look courageous.

"Oh, my! I just don't know what to say." Steven was the picture of shocked outrage. "Charles, I thought everyone knew that when one hosts a shooting party, the entertainment of the male guests is not limited to partridge or grouse! I'm sure that several of your servants will be able to buy themselves some lovely new trifles in town this week, due in large part to my generosity." With that, he turned on his heel and began to walk away.

"But wait!" Puffing, Wooldridge caught up with him, spinning Steven around by his shoulder. Red-faced, he spat out a question. "But why are they all sick? Can't even get most of their work done. It's a blasted nuisance! And what about my wife?"

Steven narrowed his eyes and just for a split second

allowed them to flash red in warning. The little man backed up an inch. Smiling slyly, Steven replied, "I'm sure I don't know why they all seem so ill. Must be I provided too much of the McElroy charm for them. As for your dear wife, she has probably taken a bit of a cold. I remember her remarking how cold her bedroom seemed of late."

He paused for a moment to see if his implication hit home. Apparently it did, because the aristocrat was rendered speechless. But he didn't confront Steven. Instead he tried to play it off. "Oh, well, can't be helped I suppose… Even servants get tired sometimes. Had a few times tiring some out myself, I dare say!" Laughing much too loudly, the three men, now quaking in their boots, retreated to the other side of the room. But Steven watched them whispering about him.

"Well, that was unpleasant," said Bernard as he adjusted his cuffs. Steven knew that Bernard would not put up with the dangerous gossip surrounding him much longer. He would soon be asked to leave their arrangement, just as he had asked others to do the same before.

Bernard asked, "Just how many maids were there?"

Squinting up at that ceiling for a moment, Steven thought about it. "Oh, six or seven, maybe eight. And the wife. I was there almost two weeks, you know. But you don't see them complaining, do you?"

This statement succeeded in making his best friend laugh. "Too true! I like to spread the joy also!"

Steven thought back on how much he had taught Bernard over the course of the three years they had roomed together. When they first met, Bernard was still killing his victims and drinking their whole reservoir, then having to stumble about at night hiding the bodies. But Steven had taught him how to take just enough every few days and how to move around the body so that teeth marks could be easily hidden.

Steven's special place for the ladies was the inside of the upper thigh. Oh, how they loved that! But he could also access the neck, upper arm, or bosom area. Once he explained to Bernard that all one had to do was find a place where the blood was close to the surface, Bernard adopted this less violent philosophy wholeheartedly. To this day, Steven had never asked him where his favored point of access was; he was too afraid he already knew.

As for the providers, as Steven thought of them, he made sure they had the best experience of their lives. It was only fair. After all, they were keeping him alive. Depending on the person, it could take them up to a week to regain their strength, sometimes longer depending on how much he took, but they never really knew what he was doing. Careful to tire them out in several ways, making sure they enjoyed it, they never sent up any alarms…as long as he left them with the promise he would be back.

But now, who to choose? He hadn't nourished for almost two days, which placed him just on the precipice of danger. Soon his hunger would overcome him and he might… Steven pushed the horrible thoughts out of his mind; he always hated killing.

Just then the scent of tropical flowers wafted over to him. Startled, he turned. Staring at him from across the room was perfection incarnate—flawless skin, deep blue eyes, hair of spun gold, and just the hint of a come-hither smile.

"Good God!" Grabbing Bernard by the shoulder, he asked, "Who is that woman?"

Bernard, who stood staring just as he was, said, "I have no idea."

Steven grabbed a waiter. "Excuse me, do you know who that lovely young woman is?"

"That's Lady Iris Visconti, m'lady's friend from Paris."

Steven moved quickly across the room. He flirted, he flattered, and in no time at all he and Lady Iris were cozied up together in the back of her carriage on their way to her London home.

As they drove, he couldn't help but notice that instead of heading towards the more posh side of town, they headed away from it. Deeper and deeper into shabby streets they drove as the fog swirled around them. They pulled up on a street desolate of buildings save one enormous old house.

"We are here, cheri!" Lady Iris spoke with delight.

"Madam, your home is quite impressive, but so out of the way. I wonder why such a fascinating creature as yourself would choose so isolated a dwelling."

They descended from the carriage and stood in front of a massive front door.

Lady Iris put her arms around Steven's neck seductively. "Cheri, I like my privacy. Here I can entertain my guests without worrying about being disturbed."

Steven dismissed his misgivings. "Probably has a jealous husband back in Paris. All the better for me," he thought.

A lanky older man opened the door.

"Thomas." Lady Iris spoke with authority. "Take monsieur to the library." She turned back to Steven, extending a dainty hand. "I must freshen up, cheri. I will be but a moment." Kissing her hand, Steven gave her a knowing look.

The older footman silently led Steven into a large, dark room where a fire still burned in the grate. He lit a few candles before he left.

Walking around the room, Steven noted the heavy velvet curtains on the windows and how much the room needed to be dusted. He stopped to admire a large, ancient-looking grandfather clock. It was a masterpiece of design, roughly six feet tall, its dark wood gleaming in the firelight. The face of the clock was beautifully hand-painted with an ornate moon dial at the top which indicated there were still at least four more hours of blessed moonlight before Steven would have to be home. The pendulum swung back and forth with such precision it was a joy to watch. The soft yet constant ticking noise soothed Steven. Turning away from the clock, he selected a book from one of the shelves. He sat in a chair next to the fire, content to read while he waited.

A moment later, the door was opened by a fresh-faced young woman wearing a maid's uniform.

"My lady said you might care for some tea while you waited." She put the tray down on an adjacent table.

Steven's hunger had been growing for hours now; he could not help but be drawn to the girl. She was wonderful—young and pretty, with the scent of lavender and fresh, innocent youth. He lowered the book just below his eyes and weighed his options. Would he have time to indulge himself before Iris returned, or would he have to wait until afterward?

The girl, uncomfortable with his wolf-like stare, shifted uncomfortably.

"What is your name, child?"

"Martha, sir."

"Martha," he practically purred. Closing the book on his lap, he fixed her with a riveting gaze.

"Have you been with Lady Iris long, Martha?"

"No, sir. Only two weeks, sir. Thomas and I were hired

by letter, and we came to get the house ready for her. She has only been in the house a few days, sir."

Steven moved so rapidly from the chair to stand beside her that she didn't even know he was there until he stroked her cheek. She jumped nervously at his touch.

"Is that lavender I smell, Martha?"

Her hand shot up protectively to her frilly cap.

"Yes, sir. I…I washed my hair today."

Clenching his fists, Steven sought to control himself. He would not wait for wooing, so close was he to her softly throbbing throat.

"Cheri, have you waited long for me?" Iris stood in the doorway, wearing only a black negligee.

In her haste to leave the room, a horrified Martha tripped as she slammed the door behind her.

Quaking with hunger and desire, Steven spanned the distance between himself and Iris in less than a second. He picked up his hostess, causing her to cry out in sudden alarm. In a moment, he had laid her down on the chaise lounge, covering her body with his. He kissed her deeply. Trying to remain lucid, he felt the unquenchable thirst rise up inside him, turning him animal-like. Fiercely he plunged his fangs into her throat. She cried out, but the noise only inflamed him more. Never had he tasted such an elixir! It was sweet and thick and peppery all at once. He drank more as she arched her back in pain and pleasure.

Out of nowhere a sharp pain hit Steven like lightning! Ripping his mouth from her, he gripped his stomach in agony and began to gag. He rolled off of her onto the floor, writhing in pain. Willing his eyes to remain open, he looked over at her.

Iris lay still, breathing in short little gasps. Gently she reached up her hand to her neck where the blood still trickled out. Catching a few drops on her fingertips, she moved them to her mouth, where she licked the blood clean. A smile began to form on her perfect lips. Slowly she turned her head towards Steven. Opening her eyes with an expression of delight and surprise, she exclaimed, "Cheri!"

Steven stared back at her in horror. There on the chaise lay a mirror image of his own features! Her eyes, like his, now glowed red. Her teeth, like his, now showed glittering fangs. She was a fiend, just as he was.

The pain shot through him again. Struggling to speak, he said, "You fool! Damn you to Hell! Don't you realize what you've done?"

Iris tilted her head to one side, blonde curls spilling around her. She began to crawl toward him like some kind of unholy beast. Steven began to scoot backwards.

"My darling, my love." She kept approaching. "To think what fate has brought us together! I have only been this way since the last full moon, and I thought I would never know another such as I. But now we are together, and we can love each other. My darling!" Reaching Steven, Lady Iris began to stroke his face with her long-nailed hands.

"No! Stay back!" Managing to sit up, still clutching his stomach, Steven felt the pressure of the bookcase on his back. "You don't understand. We cannot nourish each other—it is forbidden. Our blood is poison to each other. You have poisoned me!" Looking at her blazing red eyes, Steven realized it was almost hopeless to reason with her. So early in her transformation, she had not yet learned not to succumb to the hunger completely. The need to nourish had driven her mad.

"Cheri," Iris clucked her tongue at him like she was reprimanding a child. "I love you! I must have you!" Opening her mouth wide, she plunged her fangs into his throat. Steven screamed in pain. He had to get her off of him; she would not know when to stop, and she would drain him dry!

Iris began to tremble as she drank. Clearly the taste of such forbidden wine was intoxicating to her as it had been to him. Converting his rage to strength, he grabbed her face and flung her backwards across the room. She flew into the air, crashing against the bookcase on the opposite wall. Iris lay still on the floor, not moving. The only sound in the room was the heavy tick, tick, tick of the clock.

Standing up suddenly, she clutched at her stomach. Steven could see his blood was having the same painful, sickening effect on her. But instead of panic, her eyes shone with rage.

"I see how it is to be. You do not love me. You do not desire me! Well, we shall see what Iris will do to you, weakling. I will feed first; then I will come back to you and let you drink your fill of me!" She picked up the hem of her trailing negligee and stormed out of the room.

Gulping air, Steven tried to calm down. He needed to think! He was very weak from blood loss, and Lady Iris' blood was burning his insides. If he could get out of the house and hail a cab, maybe he could somehow make it back to Bernard. Perhaps his level-headed friend could think of some way to help him.

"Sir! Oh, sir!"

To his surprise, Martha ran into the room and kneeled beside him. Rapidly she reached up under her skirt to rip her petticoat. She pressed the cloth into his neck to try to stop the bleeding. At first Steven was confused as to why she was helping him. Then it all made sense. In his weakened state, his eyes and teeth had returned to normal. She did not see a demon-like creature, but only a handsome man, hurt and needing help.

"Martha! Dear Martha! Your mistress is a most horrible fiend! You must help me!"

"Oh, sir, I will! I heard you scream and ran to see what was the matter. That's when that…that abomination seemed to float out of the room and descend the stairs. I came in to find you so hurt! Are you all right? Will you live?"

A terrible scream rose up from all around them. The scream of a man being torn apart.

"Thomas!" Martha jerked up to run to his aide, but Steven held her down.

"No, you can't help him! It's too late!"

"Oh, sir, what are we to do?" She collapsed in his arms, weeping.

"What are we to do, indeed?" thought Steven. Now he knew why Iris had left him so suddenly. She needed to feed on something pure to try to force out the poison of his blood. Of course it would work. If it did not purge him of the vile stuff he'd drunk, it would surely slow the poison down. And here was dear Martha ready to help him in any way she could.

"My dear, let me kiss you! Let me kiss you just once, so that I might die a happy man, a man who has know the kindness of such a good, God-fearing girl." He took her tear-stained face in his hands, trying hard to seem gentle.

"But should I not run for a constable, sir? She will be back soon, I'm sure of it! Once the constable has come, you can kiss me more, if you like."

"Damn the girl for having sense," thought Steven.

"How could you find one in so dark a night with such

fog? There are no other houses to run to, and she would catch you for sure. See!" He pointed to the grandfather clock on the far wall. "It is not even time for the fishmongers to be up. No one will be about. You are safer here, hiding with me." He pulled her face closer. "Let me kiss you, just once."

Martha closed her eyes and leaned forward. Fangs out now, he angled his head towards her neck… But there, glinting in the candlelight was a silver crucifix hanging on a chain around her neck. Steven reared back in horror. He could not even look at her with that thing on.

In anguish, he turned away.

"Sir! Are you all right?" Martha, so concerned for him, leaned in closer.

Desperately trying to hide his revulsion, he choked out, "Yes, it's just the pain. Martha, you must hide—try to get upstairs and hide! You said she has not been here long. Is there some small place you could find, of which she does not know?" If he could keep Martha safe for just a little bit, it might be long enough for him to work his plan.

"Yes! There is a place behind a cupboard where she would not find me. Oh, but what of you, sir?"

Steven's sharp ears picked up a muttering from the bottom of the stairs. He slapped his hand over the girl's mouth to stop her chatter.

"Horrible old man!" Lady Iris' voice carried up to them. "You did not have enough good blood in you! Where is that chit of a girl?"

Then they both heard her calling, "Martha! Martha, where are you darling? I need to see you, cheri…"

Iris was coming back up the stairs. But the girl was his now! Steven could not let Iris drain her.

"Help me up," he whispered urgently. Martha pulled him to a standing position.

"Now, hand me that poker!" Steven braced himself against the bookcase as she ran to retrieve it for him.

When she returned, he pulled her close to him. He could feel her heart beating against his chest. Martha's big brown eyes were filled with trust.

"That's right, darling," thought Steven. "I'm your hero, come to save you. Well, save you for later, that is." Despite his pain and weakness, the thought of finishing off sweet little Martha and then ripping the head off Iris made a touch of a smile play about his lips.

"Why do you look at me so strangely?" whispered Martha.

Steven narrowed his eyes while tightening his grip on her. "Because you are so beautiful, Martha. Despite all the horrors I have seen tonight, you give me hope—hope for a long and bright future."

"You little bitch!" Iris screamed behind them. Moving so fast it again seemed as if she were floating, she ripped Martha from Steven's arms and hurled her backwards. Martha tumbled violently over the table with the tea set and lay amidst the broken china.

With a cry of rage, Steven hurled himself at Iris with the poker. It connected with her temple, causing a sickening crack. Still, Iris did not fall down. She leapt at his throat, pushing him backwards with all her might. They knocked over the chaise and crashed against the heavily curtained windows. The force of the two of them together then bounced them onto the floor, where Steven rolled out from under her in a second. Lying on his back, he kicked at her with his black boot, but she in turn grabbed his leg and jerked it so violently that he was propelled past her into the fireplace. His hand grabbed a burning log, and he held it above his head, getting ready to throw it at her when he heard Martha cry out.

Lavender-scented chestnut hair tumbling out of her cap, Martha held one hand to her mouth to keep herself from crying. Her hands and face were bleeding and torn from the broken china, but it was her eyes that looked the worst to Steven. She looked at him as if he were the devil himself! For a moment he was confused, but then he understood. Fighting with Iris, his eyes once again glowed red, his fangs dripping with saliva. She knew what he was now. She knew and she was afraid!

Knowing his horrible personage was still on display, he tried to make his voice calming. “See what she has done to me, dear Martha! You must help me!” Lowering the log, he reached out to her.

Just then Iris, who had crawled around in the dark behind Martha, burst forth, grabbing the girl by the throat. She was almost to the point of ripping apart the tender skin when Steven yelled, “Martha! The cross!” It was just enough time to stop Iris. The female fiend reared back in horror as Steven threw the log with all his might. Martha scrambled to her feet, running out of the room and up the stairs. Steven made his move, throwing the log with such supernatural force that it severed the pretty blonde head right off Iris’ body. The wood stuck in the wall like a tack holding down an insect.

Steven walked over casually, watching Iris’s headless body twitch around on the floor for a moment or two. Then, with a crumbling sound, her skin began to pop open, releasing a foul odor. After a few moments, only a thick layer of gray dust covered the floor where Iris once lay.

He sat down to catch his breath on the armrest of the one chair that still remained upright. Until that moment, he hadn’t realized how weak he was. Steven sniffed the air. No, the girl hadn’t left the house. He could still smell the lavender.

Forcing himself to stand, he stiffly walked toward the staircase. All he had to do was find the cupboard upstairs. Now, at least, he did not need to waste time on pretty words. Gazing at the tall clock, he watched as the moon dial slid forward smoothly. The clear chimes rang out four times. He needed to hurry. The pain on his insides was increasing.

Martha ran crying into Lady Iris's bedroom. Oh, how could she escape this Hell she was in? These things she had seen were the stuff of nightmares! They couldn't be real. Her grandfather had told her stories of such things to scare her. But they were real, and she had almost perished because of them.

And him—a liar the whole time! How he had lied when he said he would protect her. How stupid she had been to believe him.

Leaning against the door, Martha began to pray. She had not gone to the cupboard hiding place because she knew he would look there first. But where could she hide? Should she try to get out the front door? But she would have to run out into the open, and he moved so fast!

It would be morning soon. Hadn't her grandfather told her these unnatural things could not stand the light? A hair pin fell out of her hair onto the floor. Martha looked down at it, not seeing it at first. Then she touched her hair, thinking. As fast as she could, she ran to the dressing table and began to pull open the drawers.

Steven was growing very angry now. He had been in every room upstairs, checking in and behind every wardrobe, bed, and cupboard he could find. The pain was intensifying so much, he found it hard to walk. He struggled down the stairs, holding onto the banister.

"Martha!" he bellowed. "You know by now I have barricaded the doors. You can't get out. Just come to me, and it will all be over soon. You won't even be hurt. I can make you forget all the pain and just go to sleep. Come now, Martha! It would be so much better for you if you come to me than if I have to find you. I won't be in a charitable mood when I hunt you down!"

He stopped short. Turning his head, he drank in the scent of lavender. Somehow she had gotten past him to the first floor…the dining room. Limping quickly, he burst through the doors. Furniture covered in white sheets crowded the room.

"Martha… Come out, come out, wherever you are." He didn't really need her to come out. She was there over by the wall, huddled under a sheet. He could tell from its wrinkled state. Putting on his most charming smile, he crept over and threw back the sheet with a great flourish, only to find satchels of dried lavender stacked up under the sheet. Damn the girl! She had tricked him by using the scent to move him away from her.

"MARTHA!" he screamed.

Just then a bit of movement caught his eyes. Using the last of his lightning speed, he flew across the deep hallway and back into the library where he had waited for Iris when he first arrived. Martha, hands behind her back, stood next to the clock. She looked so frightened; it made him feel wonderful.

"Hello, dear." Steven had to hold himself up by grabbing the fireplace mantle. "Ready to help me as you so kindly promised earlier?"

Martha held out the cross necklace like a talisman. It did its job, making Steven look away quickly.

"Oh, yes. There is that. But let me tell you something, dear Martha. In my current state, self-preservation rules over disgust. Put it up again… Go ahead, hold it up." He motioned to her with one hand.

In her shaking hand she held the cross necklace toward him again. This time Steven did not turn away. Swallowing down bile, he willed himself to stare at the cross. He took all the hatred he felt and pushed it down into his inflamed gut. Somehow the power of his disgust was providing him more strength to kill her.

"See? I can fight it off. I'm still much stronger than you." The clock in the room struck five.

Steven smiled at Martha with his fangs glistening. "Oh, my. Not much time left for me to be away. Only one more hour to sunrise, so we must hurry. Now come to me, sweet little Martha, and let me kiss you as I tried before." The whole time he spoke, he moved closer to her. When he reached her, he grabbed her wrist, twisting it backwards and causing the necklace to fall harmlessly to the floor.

Pulling her toward him, Steven reached up and ripped open the bodice of her uniform.

"Please wait!" she cried.

Licking his lips, Steven replied, "Too bad you won't enjoy this as much as I will." Still holding her around the waist, he used his other hand to grab her hair. Martha hit at him with her fists. Something hard and metallic cut into Steven's forehead before it fell onto the floor.

Distracted, Steven loosened his hold on the girl just enough for her to yank herself free. Frantically she scrambled to the window and pulled back the thick curtains, flooding the room with sunlight! Steven cried out in pain as the rays touched his skin. It was only five a.m. How could the blasted sun be blazing this early?

He tried to run out of the room, but Martha ran past

him, flinging open the curtains on the other side. Turning away, he stumbled on the overturned furniture, falling down into a pool of sunlight. The pain was excruciating! He begged whatever deity was left to him for his death to be quick. His skin puckered and peeled away from his bones. He felt the fire lick every inch of him.

Martha bent down in front of him. She had picked up what had dropped out of her hand. As his skin receded from his skull, she held it out so he could see it.

It was the key to set the hour on the old clock.

You Just May Get It

By Donna A. Leahey

Abby was extremely uncomfortable. She was a little too broad in the girth to be happy sitting cross-legged on the floor. Besides that, her pants were too tight, forcing her to lean back in order to breathe, and that made her back hurt. Not only that, but there was the activity of the evening—a love-seeking spell that Megan was all worked up over.

"Come *on*, Abby!" Claudia urged, spreading her long, bony fingers wide and casting her eyes to the heavens in a plea for patience and tolerance.

"Seriously, guys?" Abby sighed.

"You have to believe, Abby, or it won't work," Megan pleaded. "And I really need it to work."

"Megan, I don't get this. You've never been into this kind of stuff."

"The girl at the bookstore told me she got a really hot guy after she and her friends did it."

"This strange girl just came up to you and started talking about doing a spell?" Abby asked doubtfully.

"No, I told you. I heard her talking to someone else, and then I *asked* her about it. She told me they did this spell and wished for hot boyfriends… And the wish came true." Megan leaned forward to whisper, though there was no one else in the apartment. "Abby, she was fatter than *me*!"

Abby frowned. "Aren't you worried about, like, evil spirits or something?"

Megan waved her hand dismissively. "Evil spirits? Don't be silly!"

"Isn't there like a 'rule of three' or something that says there's always consequences to magic?" Abby asked.

Megan's eyes cut away, and for the first time, Abby suspected she wasn't being completely honest with her. "It's perfectly safe, Abby. Come on, you've *had* a boyfriend. I really want to try this!"

Claudia turned pleading eyes on her as well. "Please, Abby?" she urged.

Abby sighed, dropped her little man-shaped token in the circle and took her friends' hands. She loved her friends; she really did. They had been her best friends since college, a friendship that had lasted through graduation, even with each of them starting to go her own way. If it would make them happy for her to sit here in front of a little fire and say a spell, she'd do it. Nothing said she had to be happy about it, though.

"Fine," she said. "Let's just do this."

It wasn't like Abby didn't understand the desire for this spell to work. She was lonely too. She hadn't had anything like a boyfriend since Jim dumped her for that stupid skinny blonde chick he'd cheated on her with. With the pounds Abby had gained around her waist over the couple of years since then, she wasn't attracting much male attention.

Megan wasn't chubby like Abby was; Megan was just plain fat and had been her whole life. She'd never had a boyfriend, possibly never been kissed. Abby thought Megan was really pretty, despite her weight problems, with beautiful thick shining blonde hair she wore long, and a face with pretty eyes, full lips, and an upturned nose. She was bright and funny, and she could sing like an angel. Unfortunately, she couldn't get past her weight in her own head and expected that no man anywhere would ever be able to get past it either. Personally, Abby thought there were plenty of fat chicks out there with boyfriends, so the fat wasn't the problem. A few years ago, some frat boys had played a cruel and humiliating prank on Megan that ended up with leaving her alone in the middle of a cow pasture. Since then, she didn't even try to talk to men outside of the School of Music where she studied for her master's degree in music and worked as a graduate assistant.

Claudia, on the other hand, was the Mutt to Megan's Jeff. She was unusually tall for a girl and skinny. But not glamorous, supermodel skinny. Claudia was bony and ungainly, with knobby knees and pointy elbows, a long face, a big nose, and an undershot chin—a look Abby had always thought of as "weasel face." She slunk around in a perpetual slouch, with her hair in her face and her eyes down. Like Megan, Claudia was extremely talented—her sketches and paintings were near photographic quality, and she had an amazing eye for color and composition.

Claudia had dated the same guy from junior high until he graduated from college. He'd convinced her to drop to part-time student so she could work and support him, promising that he'd reciprocate. Then, on the day he got his new job and big sign-on bonus, he'd dumped her. That's when her friends learned that the wonderful boyfriend had done a number on Claudia's self-esteem. She was completely convinced that no man would ever be interested in her again, and she'd never finished her degree. She worked at a non-profit putting together their newsletter, her wonderful sketches prominently featured in each issue.

Megan arranged the paper with the careful instructions for the spell on the floor in front of her, smiled hopefully at her friends, and then began to read the words aloud. Her singer's voice gave the exotic words a rich, full sound. Abby thought the syllables and rhythms sounded like Latin, but she couldn't identify any particular words. While Megan chanted, Claudia craned her neck to read the instructions and dropped assorted objects into the tiny fire burning in a brass bowl in the middle of the circle.

The flames abruptly flared up and began to burn a bright green. "Okay, okay… I go first," Megan declared, pulling her hands back from her friends. "As the caster of the spell, I mean. I go first. That's what it says on the page."

"Fine," Abby muttered.

"I ask the flames to bring me the man of my dreams. He will be blond and rich, and drive a big, red sports car. He will be handsome and think big women with curves are sexy." Megan smiled happily, took the totem she'd constructed, and tossed it into the flames. It vanished in a flash of sparks. The flames turned blue, then back to yellow. "Your turn, Claudia!"

The bony brunette clutched her totem in her hands and closed her eyes. "I ask the flames to bring me the man of my dreams. I want him to be tall, taller than me! I want… I want… tall, dark, and handsome! With a six-pack and… and a sexy accent… and a great ass!" She giggled and tossed her totem—it was a remarkable work of art, and it was a shame it went into the fire. As before, sparks rose up from the bowl. The flames burned a deep, bloody red, then slowly changed back to yellow.

"Go, Abby!"

Abby sighed and rolled her eyes. "I just want—"

"Say it right, or it won't work for *any* of us!" Megan

hissed.

Abby exhaled slowly, picked up her totem, and spoke. "I ask the flames to bring me the man of my dreams." She paused, remembering Jim and all the horribly cruel things he'd said to her after she learned about his cheating. "I just want a nice guy," she said with a shrug.

"For God's sake, Abby," Megan said. "Dream a little! Don't you want a hunk?"

Abby shook her head with a laugh. "Fine. He should have a rockin' body, dark hair, blue eyes." She glanced down at the totem in her hands and whispered, "A nice guy who loves me and won't hurt me." She held the totem over the fire and laughed. "And tattoos! I love a guy with tattoos!" She dropped the totem. The flames flared up bright blue, then faded back to yellow. A sudden cascade of sparks erupted. Then the fire sputtered out.

The three had a tradition of dinner out together every Thursday, so they met the evening after the spell. Megan drove, though she was quiet behind the wheel of her early model sedan. Abby wondered if her friend had expected the three dream men to knock on the door as soon as the spell was finished. But by the time they said their good nights, all three had to admit that it might take some time. Still, Megan was distinctly disappointed, and even Claudia, usually the most upbeat of their little group, was staring silently out the window as they drove along.

"Pizza?" Abby suggested.

"I'm not hungry," Megan muttered.

"I want Thai," Claudia offered.

"Fine," Megan sighed. "We'll go get Thai."

Megan turned left at the stoplight toward their favorite Thai place, and the three friends settled into silence. Abby quietly stared out the window as they passed a trio of hot guys staring down into the open hood of a big red car. Her neck craned as she watched the shirtless dark-haired guy bend over, displaying a flawless physique decorated with a stunning tattoo of a dragon covering a large part of his back.

Her face abruptly met the seat in front of her as the car screeched to a halt. "Holy crap, Megan!" Abby complained, sitting back up. "What was that?"

"Three guys—one tall, dark, and handsome, one tattooed, the third blond with a big red muscle car? They're *our* guys!" Megan executed a sharp turn into the parking lot and wheeled in a few spots over. The three men straightened, looking at them in the car. Abby was impressed by Megan's powers of observation. The three did, indeed, match what they'd wished for.

Unfortunately, now that they'd arrived, not one of the women had the confidence to get out and talk to the trio of handsome men. Finally, the blond man walked up to the car, a charming smile on his face. "Excuse me, ladies," he said. "I don't suppose you have jumper cables in your car, do you?"

Despite Megan's previous confidence, she hung her head, staring at her lap, and mumbled. Claudia stared, wide-eyed and open-mouthed, resembling nothing so much as a startled animal shared again and again as an internet meme. Abby blushed and stammered, "Me- Me- Megan… Open the trunk."

The blond man's eyes lingered on Megan as Abby scooted out of the car. She lifted the trunk lid and found Megan's neatly organized car safety kit under a folded blanket. Without another word, Abby handed the jumper cables over to the blond man. He smiled at her, glanced at Megan again and asked, "Can you pull over closer to my GTO, doll?"

While Megan fumbled to get her car in reverse, Abby walked over to the car, uncomfortable and unused to the way all three handsome young men were eying her. She bit at her lip nervously, especially after she noticed the shirtless guy with the dragon tattoo staring at her. His eyes were wide. His mouth hung open. It looked like someone had just hit him in the back of the head. He dropped his eyes and shook his head as if to clear it, then looked up at Abby and smiled.

"Hey. I'm Luc," he said. "What's your name?"

"Erm… Abby," she answered, awkwardly offering her hand.

Luc accepted it gently and turned his grip in hers so that he held her fingertips. He stared at her so intently that for a moment she thought he was going to kiss her fingers like in an old movie, but instead he placed his other hand atop hers and leaned in towards her. "You and your friends saved us. We're from out of town, got no one to call for help, and Nick there doesn't believe in AAA."

Her cheeks warmed, but she smiled back. The blond guy was leaning in the window close to Megan. "Go ahead and pop the hood, sweetie," he said.

The third man leaned back against the GTO, arms crossed, a tiny smile on his face, his dark eyes fixed on Claudia. He was darker than his companions, with an exotic cast to his features. It was no surprise when a hint of an accent colored his words. "Thank you, ladies, for being so kind as to stop for us," he said. He quickly skinned out of his shirt, revealing a sculpted body with a defined six-pack, and reached out his hand for the cables. "I will attach them to our lovely new friends' car, Nick."

Megan and Claudia huddled close behind Abby. Megan was whispering, "Holy shit… holy shit… it worked… holy shit…"

"I've never even *talked* to a guy this hot before!" Claudia whispered.

Within moments, the GTO roared to life. The guys high-fived each other, and Abby had a moment of regret that the handsome Luc would be gone shortly. Nick efficiently removed the cables and handed them back to Abby. "Ladies, thank you so much. Just so everyone knows everyone, I'm Nick, this is Luc, and the one who can't take his eyes off your willowy friend is Beltran, but we all call him Bel."

"I'm Abby, this is Megan and Claudia."

"Ladies, you must let us repay you for your kindness!" Nick insisted. "May we take you to dinner?"

"We… we… were just going to get Thai," Megan mumbled, staring at the ground.

"Great! We love Thai food! Lead the way!"

Bel stepped forward. "Perhaps Claudia could ride with us, in case we become separated?"

Nick laughed and shoved Luc towards the girls. "We'll trade you Luc for Claudia."

"I don't know about this…" Abby started, but Claudia wasted no time running for the big, vintage GTO. Luc, his blue eyes on Abby, had already opened the passenger door on Megan's car.

"This is a bad idea!" she whispered to Megan as she folded herself into the passenger seat. Luc squeezed into the front seat with her and, despite her misgivings, Abby enjoyed every inch of his firm muscles pressed up against her. He chatted with Megan and Abby as if they were old and affectionate friends. By the time they arrived at the restaurant, his arm was companionably across Abby's shoulders. She found she didn't mind.

The table was covered with food. Nick, with adroit handling of his chopsticks, popped a steamed dumpling in Megan's mouth while Bel encouraged Claudia to try the chicken satay. Meanwhile, Luc was listening, apparently rapt, to Abby's story about her cats.

Abby, however, was distracted by the table next to theirs, where a pair of pretty young women in expensive clothing stared and whispered. They were the type of women who made Abby feel terribly self-conscious about her thick waist and simple, straight, ash-blonde hair. It was as if they were an entirely different species, a species of beautiful people who always knew the right thing to say and had access to an endless array of fashionable, flattering clothing, while plain girls like Abby and her friends could only watch, never able to even hope to compare. The pair paid their ticket and walked away, whispering and giggling. As they left, the blonde fake-whispered in a voice loud enough to be heard through the entire restaurant, "Save the whales! Date a fat chick!"

Megan hung her head, her face pale. Nick put an arm around her. "Pay no attention to those skinny bitches," he said to her. "I *like* a woman I don't have to worry that I'm going to break when I'm in bed with her." Megan lifted her eyes to his and smiled. "Listen, ladies," he went on. "We've got a nice suite at the Marriott. Why don't you come back with us?"

Megan's eyes widened. Claudia giggled. But Abby wasn't so sure. This whole evening was surreal. Guys like this just didn't talk to girls like them, and most definitely didn't invite them back to their suite at the Marriott. "Oh, I don't know," Abby said. "I have to work tomorrow and—"

"Abby!" Claudia hissed, her brown eyes wide. "*Of course* we'll go!"

"Of course we'll go!" Megan repeated, staring raptly at

Nick.

Abby sighed. "Of course," she said. "Of course we'll go."

The suite was large and expensively decorated. It made Abby think of a luxury apartment, with a sitting area, a small office space in an alcove, and three bedrooms. Nick pulled a bottle of champagne from a full sized fridge in the kitchenette while Bel manned the bar. After a couple of mojitos from Bel's generous hand, Abby was feeling much more comfortable about their situation; she stopped wondering what three absolutely gorgeous men were doing paying attention to her and her friends.

Luc was so attentive. He asked her endless questions about her job, her family, her pets, her childhood, and then actually listened when she answered. In the meantime, Nick had convinced Megan to sing for them. She was in wonderful voice, confident and comfortable, singing old torch songs that showed off her voice to best effect. Cuddled back against the exotic Bel, Claudia was happily doodling away on some computer paper snatched from the printer in the office.

"Come sit with me, my lovely," Nick said as Megan flawlessly finished the last notes of "Why Don't You Do Right?"

Beaming with pleasure from Nick's approval, Megan was truly lovely. She settled down beside Nick, giggling with delight when he leaned over her and began to kiss her. Bel followed Nick's lead, wrapped his arms around Claudia, and began to nuzzle her neck. The skinny girl set aside her sketch and twisted in his arms to return the affection.

Luc smiled at Abby, his blue eyes shining in the dim light. "They look cozy," he said with a glance at her friends.

Abby was warm, comfortable, just a little sleepy, and so very relaxed. Without hesitation she shifted around to lean against him, purring like a cat when he wrapped his arms around her and began to kiss her neck. "This is a dream," she murmured as she traced her finger along the tattoo of the dragon's tail which wrapped around his arm. "It's not real."

"I'm real, Abby," he said into her ear. "I'm here for you."

Her eyes still unfocused, she watched as Megan and Nick rose from the couch and trailed away into one of the bedrooms. She fantasized about grabbing Luc by the hand and heading for his room, but then she glanced at her watch. "Oh no, oh shit, I have to go! Oh shit."

Part of her badly wanted to stay. When would she ever have the chance to be with a man like this again? Men like Luc didn't look at her twice, but now here he was, gazing at her with those blue eyes, twisting up her insides, making it hard to think. It wasn't like her to jump right into bed with a man, but he was so very perfect for her.

"Oh, stay just a little longer," he said softly.

She sighed, leaned back into his strong chest, and shook her head. "I can't. I really can't. Big day tomorrow." She reluctantly untangled herself from Luc and glanced over at Claudia. "Claudia? Claudia! Don't you have to work tomorrow too?"

Claudia had herself wrapped around Bel in a tangle of arms and legs and sexy, muscular man. She ignored Abby and grabbed on to Bel harder. Abby glanced down at the sketch Claudia had been working on. It was a near photographic quality portrait of the three men. Abby smiled at the sketch, admiring her friend's skill. Luc stood between the other two while the dragon tattoo came to life and lifted off his back, the bat-like wings forming a backdrop for the image. Little doodles of animals surrounded the image—bats, cats, snakes, pigs, spiders, and a pack of coyotes howling at the cartoonish scowling face of the moon. She traced her finger over the coyotes with a thoughtful frown.

"C'mon, Claudia, we have to go."

Claudia sighed and turned her face to Abby. "I do have to get the newsletter in." She shook her head sadly. "What about Megan? We can't leave Megan."

Abby glanced at her watch again, then looked at Luc. There was something predatory in his eyes that both turned her on and worried her. She shook her head and went to the door to knock on it.

"Megan? Megan? I need to go."

There was a long silence before Megan spoke. "Take my car. I'm staying here."

Abby bit her lip, a bit reluctant to say what really worried her. "Are…you sure?"

Megan laughed and said, "If he's a serial killer, I'll die happy! I'll talk to you tomorrow."

Bel was holding onto Claudia's hand as she walked over to stand by Abby. He pulled her close. "Stay, Claudia, stay." His accent made it sound like "Cloudia."

The tall girl kissed him again. "I really do have to work tomorrow."

"Then promise me you'll come back. We will be here a few more days."

"Oh, I will!" Claudia said.

"Me too," Abby said, smiling at Luc. He smiled back and blew her a kiss. The look in his eyes made her heart pound.

Abby was only a couple minutes late to work and managed to sneak in to her desk unnoticed. She'd hardly slept the night before with excitement. Now she was so distracted, she could barely remember how to answer the phone. Luc's bright blue eyes, that smile, the warmth and strength of his body as they'd cuddled together were all more real to her that morning than the phone calls and memos.

However, as the day wore on and she couldn't reach Megan, she began to pull out of her infatuated trance. While eating her bagged lunch at her desk, she called Claudia.

"Have you talked to Megan?" she asked.

"No, it just goes to voice mail," Claudia said.

A thrill of fear shot through Abby. "Oh my God, I can't believe we left her there alone with them. What were we thinking?"

Claudia was a little slow to pick up on Abby's concern. "Maybe she's still asleep? If Nick kept her up late, she probably turned the phone off."

"Maybe…"

"We already planned to go over there tonight. We'll check on her then."

Abby hoped her friend wouldn't be dead by then, but she reluctantly agreed. However, as soon as she hung up the phone, it dinged at her with a text message from Megan. "What a gr8 nite! I cant believe it!"

"R U OK?" Abby quickly texted back.

"NEVER better!!!!"

Abby frowned at the phone. No, this wasn't good

enough. She needed to hear her friend's voice. She quickly called. Her anxiety ratcheted up another notch when a man's voice answered.

"Where's Megan?" Abby demanded.

"Hi, is this Abby? That's what it said on the phone, anyway. This is Nick. Megan's in the shower."

Confronted by Nick's friendly voice, Abby's determination wavered, but she took a deep breath. "I need to talk to her. Now."

"Oh, all right, doll. Hold on." The phone went quiet for a moment. Then she heard a door open and the sound of running water. "Hey, babe. Abby wants to talk to you. Sounds important." Silence twisted out, and she heard Nick say, "Say hello to your friend, Megan. She's worried, and you need to tell her you're okay."

"Hello." Abby recognized Megan's voice, but something didn't sound right.

"Megan? Are you okay?"

"I'm okay." She paused, then continued. "I'm tired." Abby frowned at the phone. Megan sounded like a robot, completely devoid of emotion.

Abby paused, then asked quietly, "Are you free to talk? Can they hear you?"

"I'm fine. Everything is fine."

"Oooh-kayyy" Abby answered, drawing the sounds out doubtfully. "Claudia and I will come by after work with your car."

Another long silence. Abby could hear Nick's indistinct voice. Then Megan continued. "Luc and Bel want to take you two out."

"What about you?"

"Nick and I will stay in."

"Megan—"

"I need to finish my shower. Bye."

The phone went dead. Abby stared at it, full of doubt. Something was wrong, but she couldn't figure out what. Before she could really process the conversation, her phone rang again.

"Hello?"

"Abby? It's Luc. Megan gave me your number."

Despite her misgivings, her heart began to pound and her skin flushed at the sound of his warm, deep voice. "Hi, Luc."

"Megan told you about our plans? Is that okay? We thought a little dinner, a little dancing, then back to the suite to hang out."

Confronted with his sexy voice and the kind of evening she'd always dreamed about, Abby found herself stammering an enthusiastic affirmation.

"Cool. I can't wait to see you again!"

Abby could barely remember the rest of her afternoon as she vacillated between worry for Megan and excitement about her date.

Claudia drove Megan's car while Abby drove her own back to the hotel. Abby was determined to be able to leave when *she* wanted to and not be held captive by what anyone else wanted to do. Luc and Bel met them in the lobby, but Abby insisted on going up to give Megan her keys. She found Megan sitting on the couch wearing only a t-shirt and panties, cuddled up to Nick. Her eyes were flat and barely focused.

"Megan, honey… What's going on?" Abby asked, sitting next to her friend.

Nick pulled Megan in closer and said, "I wore her out." He winked at Abby, and she rather abruptly realized she didn't like him.

"I'm tired," Megan said. Her face twisted into an expression that Abby realized was supposed to be a smile. She would have been suspicious that Nick was coercing her friend, but Megan didn't look frightened or anxious.

"I brought you your keys." Abby handed the keychain over, still watching Megan's eyes until she was distracted by the beeping of her phone.

"Come ON! The guys are ready to go!" Claudia said in her text.

"I guess I'm going. Megan, did you *take* something? Are you sure you're okay?"

Megan nodded. "I'm fine."

Abby stood, still watching her friend, but finally shook her head and walked out the door as Megan hummed an out of tune melody behind her.

The evening was magical—like every dream she'd ever had of what a date could be—dinner and dancing with an attentive, extremely handsome man. Her glass was always full and she danced until she was giddy and exhausted. Claudia and

Bel gave up the dance floor entirely and spent the last half of the evening making out in a dark booth. But Abby loved to dance, so Luc led her back out onto the floor again and again.

On the drive back to the suite, Abby kept glancing over to Luc's profile, all the while listening to the moist noises and moans arising from the back seat. She was afraid to look for fear of what she might see. Luc turned to smile at her, a warm and friendly smile, though the look in his eyes was considerably hotter.

She reached out, took his hand, and with that, made the decision. Why *not* sleep with him? Not only was he gorgeous, but he was nice to her. He glanced at her again and she smiled, giving his hand a squeeze.

There was no one in sight when they returned to the suite. Claudia and Bel wasted no time vanishing as well. Abby settled on the couch and gave her best come-hither look. Luc opened the fridge behind the bar. "Beer? Wine?"

"Got any Moscato?"

He poured two generous glasses and settled down on the couch beside her. Abby cuddled up to him and he wrapped a strong arm around her. They cuddled and talked, his hand playing in her hair, her hand resting on his chest. A sharp cry came from Bel's room, and another. Abby wondered just what was going on in there. The possibilities intrigued her, and she decided she'd waited long enough. She took a deep drink of the sweet wine, then straddled Luc's hips and plunged her hands into his thick dark hair. She stared into his surprised eyes for just a moment before closing the distance between them for a kiss.

"Babe…" he marveled when she came up for air. "Where'd my shy girl go?"

"That wasn't shy; that was uncertain. And now I'm

certain."

Luc tipped his head forward to kiss her again and wrapped his arms around her waist. "All right, then," he said hoarsely. He lifted her off his lap and led her to the remaining bedroom.

Her heart was pounding and her skin felt too tight. Blood was singing in her ears. The king-sized bed looked like home as Luc gave her a gentle shove toward it. Crawling to the center of the enormous mattress, she turned back to smile at Luc, and, for just a moment, doubted her decision. His face was an unsettling combination of lust, predation, and determination. But as their eyes met, he smiled. He grabbed his t-shirt at the bottom hem and slowly lifted it up over his head, revealing inch by inch his sculpted muscles and tattoos. He was everything she found physically attractive in a man. She wondered again if she might just be dreaming.

Bare-chested, he stood with his arms behind his head, unmoving. Abby reciprocated by pulling her own shirt off, kneeling there in her lacy bra. She abruptly felt self-conscious next to his physical perfection, with flab hanging over her waistband. But if anything, the warmth in his eyes grew hotter.

"Abby…" he said, his voice thick. "I don't know…"

She crawled toward him and reached out to hook her fingers in his waistband. "Come here," she whispered and began working on his belt buckle with shaking fingers. She pulled it loose, then unbuttoned his pants and pulled down the zipper, but when she started to reach inside, he grabbed her wrists in a move too fast for her to even see.

"No…" he whispered. His eyes locked onto hers. "What is it you've done to me?" he growled. Suddenly she remembered she was alone with a man she barely knew. He shook his head, his lips pursed. The muscles in his jaw worked. "No… No!" He shook his head again, his eyes fastened on hers with an intense determination. “Abby, you have to leave.”

“What are you talking about?”

“Shhh. I can’t. I just can’t. You have to go, and don’t come back here, no matter what.” He released his grip on one of her wrists, grabbed her shirt, and shoved it at her before dragging her off the bed.

“I don’t understand!” she wailed.

“It’s best you don’t. And be quiet!”

He opened the door, took one step out, and stopped, cursing. Nick stood just outside the door, his arms crossed. “Where ya going, Luc?” he asked. His tone of voice frightened Abby even more. Megan, completely naked, sat motionless on the couch nearby, staring into space. Her skin was pale, her eyes blank.

Luc moved in front of Abby. “She needs to go home,” he said.

“Oh, does she?” Nick drawled. “When things seemed to be going so well between you two.”

“Get out of my way.”

“You think I don’t know what’s going on?” Nick said.

Abby stepped closer to the doorway. “Luc? What is this?” she whispered.

“Bel!” Nick called. “We seem to have a problem.”

Without a word, Luc reached back and took Abby’s wrist in a firm grip, pulling her tightly against his back. Moments later, Bel stepped out of his room, wearing only a pair of shorts. “What is it?” he asked irritably. Then his eyes fixed on Abby and Luc. His brow furrowed.

"Are you finished with yours?" Nick asked.

"Oh yes," Bel said with a laugh, "though I wouldn't mind another go."

"Bring her on out, then."

" Get ready to run," Luc whispered.

As Bel turned back into his room, Luc suited action to words, leaping into motion and dragging Abby behind him. By that time, she was frightened enough that running seemed like exactly the right thing to do. She clung to his hand and raced after him, her breath hitching in her throat as she struggled not to sob with fear.

Nick beat them to the door, cutting them off. His expression was friendly, but his eyes were dark. "I don't think so, Luc. I'm already tired of this world. Finish it so we can all go home."

Bel emerged again, and when Abby saw her friend trailing behind him, she cried out, "Claudia! What did you do to her?"

Claudia was every bit as dazed as Megan, but there were fresh bruises on her face and body. Blood dripped from her nose and the corner of her mouth.

"Our friend Bel likes to hurt girls, I'm afraid," Nick said. "But not to worry, she's not feeling it anymore. Or, rather, she's not aware that she's feeling it."

"Oh my God, what's happening?"

Luc pulled Abby behind him as Nick sneered. "You all got the men of your dreams."

A chill shot through Abby. How could he know about that spell? "Claudia didn't dream for a man to beat her up!"

"Then she should have specified that. You, on the other hand, were a bit too specific—hence, our current problem."

"What are you *talking* about?" she screamed.

Nick began to talk again, but it was Abby's own voice that came from his mouth: "A nice guy who loves me and won't hurt me."

Luc cursed. At least, she thought he was cursing; she couldn't understand the language. She began to cry, hot tears rolling down her face. "I don't understand. What did you do to my friends?"

"You and your friends summoned us," Bel said. "She was warned that magic is never free, never without consequence, but she was unconcerned. So, you cast a spell which summoned us in the forms you specified. As soon as that desire is consummated, we consume your soul."

"What? No, no…" Abby shook her head. "No, that's not possible. You've just drugged them or something."

"It's true, my love," Luc said. "Their souls are gone. They will live on, a few weeks, maybe a few months, and then just…stop."

"They're going to die?"

"I believe you meant to say 'we,'" Nick commented. "As soon as Luc fucks you, your soul will be lost as well, and then the three of us can leave this world and wait for the next trio of foolish, lonely girls to try the spell."

"I won't do it," Luc said.

"Yes, yes… You love her." Nick sighed. "Bel?"

Abby hadn't noticed Bel moving, but he was now close enough to grab at her. Luc stepped between them, pushing

Abby back with his hip. She screamed, then screamed again as an enormous sword, apparently made entirely of fire, appeared in Luc's hands.

Nick sighed and lifted his hands as fire surrounded them. Bel raised his arm as a long whip, also made of fire, sprung into existence. "Do you really want to do this, Luc? Two against one… Your love there will surely be injured, and you'll lose."

"I won't take her soul." He turned to face Nick, brandishing his sword.

"Put your damn weapon away!" Nick demanded.

"I can't." He shook his head. "I know it's just the spell, but I can't." He laughed bitterly. "I love her."

Abby had only a moment's warning as the flaming whip flashed through the air. Then she screamed with pain unlike anything she'd ever felt as it wrapped around her wrist. Bel jerked at the whip and dragged her away from Luc, wrapping his left arm around her body and holding her tight.

At the sound of her scream, Luc roared furiously. "Let her go!" he demanded.

"Luc, my brother," Nick said, shaking his head. "This isn't your fault. It's that bitch and her wish making you behave this way. We understand…we do. So, here's what's going to happen. You're going to take her body and her soul, and then this spell will be broken and we'll have our friend back."

"I said I won't."

"Bel will hurt her. Bel will keep on hurting her until she begs you to do it."

As if to emphasize the point, Bel grabbed Abby's burned wrist and squeezed, making her scream again. Terrified, confused, and in pain, she began to sob. Luc raised his sword but Bel squeezed harder, twisting the burned tissue. "Scream, bitch!" he whispered in her ear, and she complied.

"Stop hurting her," Luc said flatly. His burning sword vanished. "Take her to the bedroom, and we'll finish this."

"No, no, wait!" Abby cried, but Bel was already dragging her through the narrow door.

"Trust me, Abby, this is what's best," Luc said, holding her eyes.

"Fuck you!" she screamed, struggling futilely to get free.

"That's the idea!" Nick laughed as he grabbed at Abby as well and pulled her back onto the bed. They were too strong to be human; she was as helpless as a babe in their hands. Luc stood at the foot of the bed, his head down, his hands working open and closed, while Nick and Bel pushed her down despite her struggles and screams.

"Well?" Bel demanded. "Get on with it!"

"She's still wearing her pants."

"I cannot wait for this spell to be over," Bel grumbled as he bent down to unbutton Abby's jeans while Nick tugged at the waistband. As soon as their eyes were off Luc, the flaming sword reappeared. With one blinding fast motion, the sword cut through the air. Bel's head fell off his shoulders onto Abby's belly. Blood fountained up from the stump of his neck as his knees buckled and his body collapsed to the floor. Nick jumped back. Abby, finally released, scrambled off the bed into the corner of the room. Luc and Nick were between her and the door, leaving her trapped until they moved.

Nick stared at his fallen friend with stunned eyes. "You killed him! Luc, you *killed* him!"

"And you're next!" Luc growled.

"Oh, Luc. When this is over, you're going to regret that."

Luc gave a bitter laugh. "He hurt Abby. I will never regret killing him for that."

"You imbecile! It's just the spell!" Nick began to move, circling the edge of the bed.

"I don't care. I love her. I can't stand by and let her be hurt."

"If you don't take her soul, we're both trapped here. Forever! I'd kill her myself if not for that. So, let me be clear. You're going to take her soul. I'm not staying in this filthy world another minute longer than I have to!"

Abby screamed as fire began to fly around the small room. Her burned wrist hurt badly, but she hardly felt it now that she was faced with the prospect of being burned alive. She pressed herself back into the corner, whimpering.

Luc and Nick danced around the small room. The flaming sword swung in huge arcs while Nick flung fireballs that exploded into blazing fires wherever they struck. The curtains were already ablaze, the bed skirt as well. One of the chairs was a melted ruin, and another smoldered vigorously.

Abby cowered in her corner, trembling with terror, faint with pain, eyes focused on the two demons. Nick drove Luc back, and back again, until the doorway was clear. Luc's eyes cut to her and back to the door, and she realized he'd deliberately fallen back to allow her escape. As soon as she was certain she could, she darted across the room and out the door. Nick made a grab for her, but Luc slashed at his extended wrist and Nick snatched his hand back moments before losing it.

"Run, Abby!" Luc called.

Abby raced to her friends. Megan was still and silent, but Claudia was scribbling a shapeless blob on the surface of the coffee table. Both were compliant and willingly followed Abby once she took their hands. Heedless of their nudity, she led them straight out the suite's main door and raced for the elevator. As they passed a housekeeping cart, Abby grabbed clean sheets and draped them over her friends' shoulders. When the elevator doors opened at ground level, she dragged them through the lobby, ignoring the calls of hotel staff.

Free of worry for Abby's safety, Luc pressed his attack. His sword moved like an extension of his arms, knocking away Nick's fiery attacks and pressing him back.

"Luc, stop!" Nick protested. "You don't want to do this!"

"You hurt Abby," Luc growled, pushing Nick back.

"It's the spell, Luc!" Nick held up his hands in a gesture of peace.

Luc paused to hear him out. "I know it, but knowing doesn't stop it from working on me."

"Just do it, Luc. Just finish this and we can be done."

"I will *never*!" He shifted his sword, bringing it to bear on Nick.

"Then after I finish with you," Nick's hands erupted into flames again as his voice rose, "I'll kill her myself. If I'm going to be trapped here forever because of her, then she will be begging me to kill her before I finish with her!"

"You will not touch her!" Luc twirled his sword

overhead, charged forward, and plunged it into Nick's chest. With a savage twist, he yanked the sword out before Nick had even begun to react and swung downward with all his might. The sword cleaved through drywall and colorful wallpaper, and sliced Nick's upper body from right shoulder to left chest.

As his friend fell in a cascade of surprised blood, Luc turned away. Head down, posture defeated, he strode out of the now blazing bedroom and into the sitting area. There on the coffee table he spied Claudia's sketch of Luc with Nick and Bel. He shook his head, full of grief, and picked it up.

Abby's eyes were puffy, swollen, and shiny with tears as she returned home. Claudia had lasted only four days before wasting away to nothing more than a wan, fragile skeleton, and dying. Megan was wasting away too, but she had reserves Claudia never had. Still, the mystified doctors didn't expect Megan to last another week.

She stepped into her house, but even the raucous greetings of her three cats elicited only the tiniest smile. She started to pet them, then noticed an envelope lying there on the floor. She frowned at the unfamiliar handwriting spelling out her name.

Inside were two pieces of paper. The first read simply, "I thought you might want this, as a memento of your friend." Her gut dropped just as if she were on a roller coaster. She didn't want to look that second paper, yet she had to.

Fingers trembling, she unfolded the page and saw Claudia's last drawing—the three handsome young men, surrounded by the wings from the dragon tattoo rising from Luc's back and by the little doodles of various animals. She gasped and dropped the paper. Not because of what Claudia drew, but because of the words added at the bottom.

I will watch over you.

Forever.

— L.

PINOCHI OH!

by L.A. Smith

"Come on, Oak!"

"Don't be a pussy, Oak!"

"What's-a-matter, Oaky? Scared?"

Pinocchio stood outside the gap in the chain link fence that surrounded the recently closed amusement park. The other boys had already gone through and were standing on the other side waiting impatiently for him.

"I don't know, guys. My Dad told me to come straight home. He'll worry about me if I'm late."

"Lame! That is so lame, dumbass!" Roy said. He was the leader of the group and wherever he led, the others followed.

Pinocchio was a very recent follower. Until now, it had been easy and fun, a bunch of guys hanging out and playing the odd prank on someone. No real harm in that. Boys will be boys. This was different though. The condemned amusement park looked…ominous. Pinocchio had a bad feeling about it.

Roy turned to go. "Come on, guys, he's not coming. Oaky's a chickenshit."

The others followed suit and were soon chanting "chickenshit" in unison.

"Stop it! I'm not!" Pinocchio yelled. "I'm not afraid!"

Bad idea. It was a lie. He *was* afraid. His already freakishly long nose grew a fraction of an inch longer. He could feel it. It itched. He refused to scratch it, trying desperately not to draw attention to it, hoping no one would notice. Unfortunately, his new friends were aware of his affliction and kept a close eye on his "tell."

"Hey, I think Oaky's nose just got a little longer!" Jimmy yelled.

Much laughter and further taunts ensued.

"I think you're right, Jimmy. I bet it's bigger than your dick now!"

"Fuck you, Andy. You wish your dick was that big."

"Bet Oaky wishes his was," Ben said.

"Man, I wish my dick grew every time I lied. I'd be lying all the time!" said Joe, grabbing his crotch.

Roy intervened. "Shut up, dumbasses!" He looked at Pinocchio again. "You coming or not?"

Pinocchio looked around and shrugged. "I'm coming. But just for a little bit."

The amusement park had been shut down for a while. It

looked like a ghost town movie set, all the buildings closed up, several shutters askew. There was no mistaking the smell though. The odor of fried food and garbage still clung to the place, whispering "carnival." Pinocchio half expected to find crowds of thrill-seeking ghosts around every corner, but all was quiet.

After climbing like monkeys on motionless rides for a bit, Roy led his band of followers to an old clapboard cafeteria, its garish paint job faded and peeling. It was shut up tight, the large wooden shutters closed and locked over every window. Roy tried the door but didn't seem surprised when it failed to open. He stepped back and kicked at the handle. The wood cracked. Another couple of kicks and the door flew open. The boys filed into the dark building.

Someone found the light switch and flipped it. The electricity was still connected, but only a few bulbs were intact, providing just enough light to navigate the layout of tables and chairs.

"What are we doing in here?" Jimmy asked.

"I'm hungry," Roy answered. "Might still be food in here somewhere."

"Cool!" Joe said. "Let's go raid the kitchen.

Pinocchio hung back as the others ran the length of the room and invaded the kitchen. He wasn't interested. Wooden boys didn't eat. Not even magically mobile ones. Sighing, he pulled a chair away from the table and sat down. Folding his arms on the table top, Pinocchio bent his head toward them, only to find the way impeded by the length of his nose.

"Darn."

Scooting further away from the table, Pinocchio once more lowered his head to his arms, his nose now hanging off the edge of the table. He wondered if his Dad was worried about him. Probably so. He'd never been out this late before. Lifting his head, Pinocchio glanced at the open doorway. It was getting dark. He shouldn't have come. He should have been a good boy and gone straight home. Why was it so hard to do the right thing?

Pinocchio looked towards the noisy kitchen. Hopefully the others would soon get bored with their destruction and they could leave. Sighing again, he once more dropped his head to his arms and lost himself in misery.

It was the smell that stirred him from his thoughts. He hadn't paid much attention to the shuffling noise, assuming it was merely one of his ne'er-do-well companions. But the smell—the overpowering stench of week-old road kill on a hot day—that smell made Pinocchio look up. He stared in shock at the group of rotting corpses slowly making their way single file toward the kitchen. Noticing his movement, a couple of the walking dead glanced his way, gave a sniff and walked on, ignoring him.

Pinocchio jumped up, knocking his chair to the floor, and ran to the other side of the room. His back to the wall, he stared at the grotesque procession in mute terror. More undead were still filing in, blocking his escape. The one in front had almost reached the kitchen. Oh no! The kitchen! His buddies were in there!

Panic spurring him into action, Pinocchio sprinted towards the kitchen, yelling.

"Guys! GUYS!"

The mobile corpses had gained a head start while Pinocchio sat wallowing in self-pity. The one in front was going to reach the door to the kitchen before him!

Grabbing a chair, Pinocchio swung it wildly as he charged the zombie at the head of the procession. It connected, and the dimwitted dead man crashed into his necrotic companions behind him. They fell like dominoes and Pinocchio, taking advantage of the momentary confusion, rushed into the kitchen. His buddies were oblivious to the danger that was coming for them, happily emptying the contents of the cupboards in search of something that might possibly be edible.

Jimmy was the first to notice him. “Hey, Oak, decide to come join in on the fun?”

Slamming the door behind him, Pinocchio turned to his friends, wide-eyed. “We gotta get out of here! There are dead people out there and they’re trying to get in here!”

His exclamation was met with silence and slack faces for about three seconds before the boys erupted in laughter.

“Shut the fuck up!” Ben grinned.

“What are you on about, Oak?” Joe asked.

“Good one, Oaky,” Jimmy snorted.

Pinocchio stared uncomprehending at his friends, failing to see how they could not understand the gravity of the situation until he realized just how crazy it sounded. Thankfully, or maybe not, he was saved from explaining by a loud thump on the door he was leaning against.

They boys’ grins fell from their faces, and they all jumped when the noise came again, louder and with such force that it made Pinocchio bounce.

“Someone’s out there!” Ben whispered loudly.

The thumping and bumping continued.

Roy stepped up to Pinocchio,“Who’s out there?”

“Dead—” Bump. Bounce. “—dead people!”

"Liar! Who is it?" Roy growled.

"I told you! Dead people!"

"I'm gonna kick your ass if you don't—"

"Roy! Oak's nose. It's not growing," Jimmy said. "Look! He's not lying."

Sure enough, Pinocchio's tell was telling the truth. His nose had not lengthened even a fraction of an inch—which meant there really were dead people on the other side of the door, or what Pinocchio perceived as dead people. Either way, it wasn't good.

"Shit! What do we do now, Roy?" asked Ben.

"We gotta get out of here!" shouted Joe as he dropped a box of stale cookies and darted towards the only other door in the kitchen. It wouldn't budge. He panicked. "It's locked! We're trapped! We're all gonna fuckin' die!"

"Joe, chill!" Roy yelled.

A loud crack came from the door Pinocchio was struggling to keep closed. He was being bounced and bucked by the battering the door was taking, and it sounded like it had almost reached its breaking point. "Uh, guys?"

Roy took charge. "Come on, let's get this back door open. It's just wood. It shouldn't be too hard to break it down."

The boys, with the exception of Pinocchio, put their shoulders to work and in unity threw themselves at the locked door. The door cracked and splintered. Ben's shoulder broke through, and a jagged piece of wood sliced through his shirt and skin like a knife. He screamed and fell to the floor. Blood quickly started pooling at his side.

"Jesus," Joe gasped.

"Don't touch it!" Ben yelled as Roy knelt beside him.

The wound was very bad. It started as a small scratch above Ben's elbow and gradually deepened as it made its way up to his shoulder, where it gaped open, revealing bloody meat.

"I'm not gonna fuckin' touch you, asshole," Roy said. "I just wanted to see how bad it is. You gonna be able to come with us?"

Ben took a look at Pinocchio, who was still riding the waves of the rippling door. "Well, I sure as hell ain't staying here." He sucked in a breath and pushed himself up with his good arm, grimacing at the pain. Jimmy took his shirt off and wrapped it around Ben's arm to slow down the loss of blood.

Roy dashed over to the big stove and grabbed a huge cast-iron skillet. He attacked the hole in the door, knocking away the jagged pieces. Joe and Jimmy helped by kicking at the lower edges. In less than a minute, the way was clear.

"Time to go. Oaky, come on," Roy said.

"You guys go first. I'll follow. I don't think they're interested in me. They walked right by me in the dining room."

Roy nodded and squeezed through the broken door. Ben was helped through. Jimmy was next. Joe was last. He beckoned to Pinocchio. "Let's go, Oak!"

Pinocchio left his post and dashed through the jagged doorway. He could hear the door crash open behind him, but he didn't look back.

Outside the cafeteria, the sun was setting. It had already gone behind the other buildings that crowded the midway of the abandoned carnival. Darkness was falling. Death was following.

Pinocchio saw the other boys heading for their exit and

ran after them. Ben stumbled and slowed down, but Jimmy grabbed him and helped him along. Movement off to the side caught Pinocchio's attention. He turned his head to see several figures lurching towards them.

"Roy!"

Roy had already stopped. Several of the walking corpses were blocking his path. He turned to look at his followers, and Pinocchio was shaken by the fear he saw on their fearless leader's face.

The fence where the boys had entered the park was close enough to see, despite the growing darkness. It could have been on the other side of the park for all the good its proximity did them though. Their way was blocked. Pinocchio looked around for another means of escape and found none. Every direction he turned, there were dead people shuffling towards them, getting ever closer.

They were going to get massacred. He was sure of it. Creepy, walking dead people didn't chase you down to give you hugs and kisses. They came after you to tear you apart, piece by piece, and to eat those pieces with great gusto.

Unless you were made of wood.

"Come on, guys, follow me!"

Prying loose a piece of wood trim hanging from a nearby abandoned booth, Pinocchio ran toward their exit. Swinging his makeshift weapon like a baseball bat, he quickly dispatched the closest obstacles, a couple of especially rotten corpses. Their skin burst like overripe melons, juicy and full of pulpy entrails. Gore flew everywhere.

Roy and the boys followed Pinocchio as he hacked their way to safety, occasionally getting struck by flying, fetid flesh. They dared not lag behind. The dead were closing in faster than Pinocchio was making a path.

“They’re coming,” Jimmy yelled.

“Oak!” Roy urged.

There were too many of them. Pinocchio had taken out at least a dozen, but they just kept coming. He concentrated on the few remaining corpses between himself and the gate. SMACK! Three left. CRUNCH! Two left. SPLAT! One left.

“Aaahhhh! Help me!”

Pinocchio turned to see Jimmy and a zombie engaged in a tug of war, with Ben as the rope.

“Oh my god! Please! No!” Ben screamed.

Jimmy was losing.

“Aaaaahhhh! He’s eating me! Help me!”

Another corpse joined the winning side, and Jimmy was forced to let go. Ben fell to the ground and was lost to sight as the hungry dead fell upon him, devouring him like a swarm of locusts.

“Fuckin’ hell!” Jimmy exclaimed.

When the zombie he’d turned his back on bumped into him as it walked past, Pinocchio woke from his shock, raised his club and brought it down upon the dead head with all he had. The wood embedded itself in bone and brain, and the walking corpse went down.

The way was free! But it wouldn’t be long before the gap would close.

“Guys, come on!”

Roy, Jimmy, and Joe were quick to turn away from the writhing mound of zombies and run for the fence with Pinocchio. They hadn’t got far when Joe stumbled, his foot catching on one of the fallen zombies. He lost his balance and fell down.

"Help!"

Pinocchio stopped and turned to see one of the corpses closing in on Joe as he struggled to get up. His friend wasn't going to make it. He had to save him.

"You guys go through the fence. I'm gonna get Joe."

Pinocchio rushed to rescue his fallen buddy. The zombie had already thrown himself on Joe, who was on his back kicking and fighting as hard as he could, barely managing to keep his parts away from the hungry, gnashing mouth.

Not slowing down, Pinocchio barreled into the zombie, knocking it off his friend.

"Go!"

Joe jumped to his feet and took off, Pinocchio close behind. He'd only gone a few feet when he started feeling dizzy. He slowed and shook his head.

"Oak, come on!" Jimmy yelled.

He tried to run again. Something wasn't right. He felt so…strange. He looked up to see Joe reach the fence and squeeze through the hole. It wasn't far. Just a little farther. He could make it.

"Oaky, what's the matter? Come on!" Roy urged.

"I'm… I'm coming."

Lurching like one of the walking dead behind him, Pinocchio made his way toward the fence. What was happening to him? He didn't feel like himself. He…he *hurt.* He'd never hurt before. Wooden boys didn't feel pain.

A crowd of corpses were right behind him. He could smell them. Hear them. They were moaning and grunting and…sniffing.

Pinocchio finally made it to the chain link fence, his hands reaching out and grabbing it for support. They weren't his hands though. The hands that gripped the fence tightly were flesh and blood. And despite the filth and gore that covered them, they were beautiful.

"I'm a real boy," he whispered. He looked at his friends, who were backing away from him in horror, and held his new hands out for them to see. "I was a good boy."

The zombies fell on him.

He was a tasty boy.

The Drowning Man

By M.A. Chiappetta

I wake up soaked and covered in seaweed.

The icy air prods my starved, chilled limbs as though the winter goddess has dragged me to her lair to ply me with her killing wiles. Weighed down by freezing darkness, I choke, then roll onto my side and cough out water.

Oh gods of earth and sea. I must have drowned again. A man is not meant to endure such madness.

Exhausted, I lie shuddering and naked on the shore, my eyelashes gritty with sand, lips tinged with the sharp bite of salt. I curl up to warm myself, like the babe born to my wife and me not long ago. The memory of his newborn fingers rounded into baby fists is like fire in my heart. It sends heat through my limbs. Stokes my anger. And while the last thing I desire is to return to the smothering water, as soon as my strength returns, that is exactly what I will do. Again and again. I have no choice.

I must save my infant son, who lies cradled in a witch's embrace deep within the heart of the sea.

He is not dead, no. That would be a kindness, for the watery grave is no place for a living child to dwell. The sea's embrace is cold, dark, and crushing. No warmth. No mother's love. No father's strength. Only emptiness and a terrifying silence.

Who will tell my boy he is loved, if I do not find him? If I do not tear him from the ocean's depths and carry him to the sandy shore where men can surround him with strong, comforting arms and speak hope into his frail soul?

I cannot abandon him.

Ignoring the slow ache in my muscles, I push myself to my knees, my soaked hair tangled over my eyes as though to keep me blind. To my left, waves crash violent and screeching, water thinning and reaching toward me, but stopping on the sand several hand-spans away. The wind shrieks through the reeds. The sea-witch is chanting, trying to frighten me back to my hut.

The thought of the small thatched roof, the reed-covered floorboards, draws my eyes to my right, past the boundary wall, where my home sits darkened and slowly falling into disrepair. I swear I smell the rich, brown gravy of a lamb stew, spiced with treasured herbs fresh from the market day pickings. The savor of it rises on my tongue, taunting me. My wife had cooked like no one else I knew. So gifted. So lovely. Taken from me so very young.

Rubbing away tears, I turn my gaze back to the raging sea, where the hateful witch abides. A cruel creature, she has no heart, no soul, no wisp of human kindness. No wonder my wife, also born of the sea but bright and full of life as the midday sun, fled to the shore. To me.

As I stare at the waves, I imagine my wife's body floating upon them the day I gave her to the sea for burial. The memories wrap around me like seaweed and draw me down. My beautiful Ella. I'd promised to protect her. But I could not stanch her bleeding that terrible day. There was so much blood. Too much. As my Ella's life ebbed, my son wailed as newborns do, lusting toward the light of day. He belonged to the shore. To the sun. To me.

And then the sea-witch came to my door. Somehow, she knew her daughter was dead.

After the witch lifted the babe from my dead wife's cold arms, she pointed a shell-covered finger at me, her eyes alight with a watery green glint.

"Be cursed," she said, "to live without love."

A wispy red cloud arose in the room, like the sky that sailors see when a storm is brewing. Right outside my hut's door, lightning flashed and cracked. Blinded, I fell to my knees, hands covering my face. My ears pounded from the echoes of the thunderbolt. When I could finally see and hear again, my son was gone. The witch had swept him from the hut like the waves sweep back into the sea and fled to where I could not find her.

I did not even have time to name him.

Maddened by what had happened, I ran outside and screamed into the twilight, praying that the witch would hear me. And understand.

"I never stole your daughter! She came to me," I shouted, fists curled as if I could fight nature to gain a second chance at everything. "She came to me and I loved her!"

My words dissipated like dying clouds in the shadowy night air. Like hope dying. My heart crumbled within me. Frantic, I cried out again. "I would have died for your daughter, would have bled in her place if it might have saved her." I broke down into bitter tears. "You cursed me, but it's too late. She's gone. I am cursed already!"

For days, I waited upon the shore for a response. For a word of forgiveness. For hope. It never came.

And so I am thrice-cursed. I have no son. I have no wife. I have no future.

Yet I rise as I have done so many times before. I have stopped counting my efforts. The sea waits for me, calling to me, speaking in my dead wife's voice.

I am fond of the shore, Ella whispers in my memory. *It is warmer than the sea and my mother's arms.*

My son now lies clutched in those arms. He needs warmth more desperately than the daughter of a sea-witch ever could.

I stumble to the water's edge. As I step in, the waves envelop my limbs, welcoming me like an old lover. I walk until I am up to my neck. After one last glance at the shore, at my hut, at the sky's night face with its stars glinting like watch-fires, I plunge beneath the surface. Wincing against the cold, I swim down, down, deeper and darker with every stroke and kick.

Maybe this time I will rescue my son before I am drowned and cast back onto the shore again. I think of Ella and pray for her memory to give me strength.

And I plunge deeper, hoping.

The Teller of Stories

By Margaret Perdue

I have always been a teller of stories.

Blessed by varied life experiences and doubly blessed by my Irish ancestors, the ability to tell a good story has always come easy for me. And people love my stories as much as I love to tell them! I have told hundreds—all true—with just the right embellishment in just the right places.

But there is one story I do not often tell, one so wonderful, strange, otherworldly, and special that I save it for only the most extraordinary people I encounter. I record it here because, in my advanced age, I have begun to feel the shadow of my mortality bearing down on me. As they say, nothing lasts forever…and it's getting very unpleasant, this whole aging business.

So, pen to paper now. No more dawdling!

It was the summer of my twenty-first birthday. My parents, having finally succeeded in securing the college diploma of their fourth and final child—me—decided to celebrate by taking the entire family on a trip to London, England. For two weeks, my siblings and I explored this fairy tale land across the pond. It was glorious! There is, in my opinion, no place more magical than England. It is so old, and everyone's soul seems so ancient, yet so full of life at the same time. I was raptured by it all.

When the time came to head back home, I knew I could no more get on that plane than I could shoot myself to the moon. My family protested, of course, but they were used to my headstrong ways, and no doubt weary from them, so they didn't put up much of a fight. My kindly father made me swear to only one request: I must get a job. I suppose the idea of my panhandling next to the Thames was too frightening for him.

Armed with enough money for two weeks only, I set off to seek employment. It was so difficult! It seemed that no business in the whole breadth of London town had any need for a tall, lanky American girl with a brand new liberal arts degree and no work experience at all. Finally, facing the next to last day of my two week deadline, I found an ad that looked promising.

It read:

Wanted. Part-time promoter for traveling arts company.

Must have good verbal skills and be willing to travel.

Serious inquiries only.

Apply in person at the Hanover Theater on Oxford Street.

I practically ran to the interview. Surprisingly to me, I was hired on the spot. I was to be the promoter for The Summerford Troupe, a group of performers based out of the Hanover, but that spent most of the summer and all of the fall traveling to smaller communities putting on plays. My job was to speak at ladies groups, primary schools, and town council meetings drumming up business. My rate of pay was slightly above volunteer work, but my room and board and most meals were paid for. For me, it was perfect. I would get to explore all of England—for free!

At this point in my narrative, I would like to introduce the members of the troupe, who stay near and dear to my heart these many years later. There were Alistair and Lydia, an older married couple who had met years earlier when they both were in the theater. They married, survived the war, raised three successful children, and had scads of grandchildren. When they were both in their late sixties, they decided to get back onto the stage together. Alistair was always telling stories of the old days, while Lydia had a knitting compulsion. She was forever making colorful scarves for everyone she knew.

Then there were Alice and Harry; ingénue and leading man, respectively. Harry was very handsome and charming, but only a marginal actor at best. He hardly ever remembered his lines. But the housewives and teenage girls he appealed to were in awe of him. Alice was simply the most beautiful girl I had ever seen. She was small and blonde, with eyes that glowed violet. At her best, she was warm and funny and generous to a fault, but at her worst, she was spiteful and cruel and often acted like a spoiled brat.

Then there was Mike P—a Scot through and through. Incredibly tall and broad shouldered, Mike was a gentle giant.

Finally, there was the man himself, Billy Summerford! At 37 years old to my 21, he seemed to me so wise and sophisticated. Billy was over six feet tall, very lean and muscular. His hair was golden blonde. His eyes twinkled with emerald green good humor as his kindly soul shone through them. Graduating early from Cambridge, he had studied only the classics; his mind was as sharp as a knife's point.

One of his greatest achievements was he had once been one of the lead actors in the Royal Shakespeare Company. Oh, yes! Billy had played all the important parts—Hamlet,

Macbeth, Caesar, Romeo. One reviewer had even gone as far as to say when Billy was onstage, it was as if the Bard himself was before us.

But despite all this fame and good fortune, Billy Summerford had different dreams. Not for him was the life onstage, oh no. He much preferred the backstage. With the aid of a few wealthy benefactors, Billy formed The Summerford Players with the intent of bringing great theater to the smaller towns and hamlets which could least afford to see it any other way. So handsome, so intelligent, so noble… How could I not have loved him? Not that I ever told him, of course.

There were others in the troupe, lots of them, for at our largest we numbered well over forty people. All of them good and kind and fun-loving. It is not to speak ill of them that I say they all fade now in my memory. Blurry and indistinct, names and faces fall away from me. But I remember all too well how they made me feel—young, loved, and wildly happy!

Oh my! Glancing back on what I have written so far, I dare say I may be meandering a bit too long on descriptions. So now, on with my story.

We had a regular schedule that we stuck to most times: Arrive in town in the early morning, set up and promote ourselves for an evening performance, perform a play that was either set down by Billy beforehand or requested by the townsfolk sometimes, then a cast party at the local pub or meeting hall, sleep in until after 11 o'clock, then on the road again the whole next day. We had been at it for a few months when we found ourselves way up north, close to the Scottish border. The night before, Harry and Alice had performed one of their best roles as Romeo and Juliet, due in no small part to a burgeoning romance between them. I thought it was all so romantic, but the others of the troupe whispered amongst themselves that no good would come of it.

That morning, Mike and I found ourselves alone in the inn's dining room, the first ones up.

"Did you hear about the row between Harry and Alice last night?" he asked me as I sat down to pour myself some tea.

"No, I went to bed right after the play. I was tired." I didn't want to tell him that I went to my room to pick out something to wear for my next day appointment with Billy to go over some promotion material. Once or twice a month he asked to meet with me, and I guarded that private time with him like a golden treasure.

"It were awful!" The big man was clearly delighted to tell me all about it as he slapped butter on a scone. "Harry shows up with some pretty little thing on his arm and starts dancing with 'er, getting all lovey-dovey. All the while, Alice is weeping and saying she's gonna quit the company, take the next train back. Poor ol' Lydia trying to get her all calmed down. But then it were the Old Man himself who had to take to comforting her, if you know what I mean." Mike bit into his scone lasciviously.

I remember feeling as if the floor had fallen out from under me. Billy and Alice? It couldn't be!

As if the universe had read my thoughts, Mike motioned for me to look out into the hallway. There was Billy, fully dressed, speaking softly to Alice, who wore nothing but her bathrobe. She had her arms around his neck in a very suggestive way while she glanced about, obviously trying to look as if she was not trying to call attention to the two of them. Billy smiled as he playfully pushed her away.

I put my head down to stare intently at my tea as he sat down at the table. At the same moment, Lydia joined us.

"Good morning, all," she said as she bundled her overfull knitting bag under the table.

"Morning, Mike, Pegs." Billy pulled my ponytail playfully.

"Morning," I muttered, not daring to look up at him. Suddenly I was sure I was going to cry. Hurriedly I got up from the table, making some excuse about forgetting something in my room. I fled the dining room, but instead of going upstairs I turned and went outside. Half stumbling, I rounded the corner of the inn, seeking only to be alone in my grief.

"You'll need this, dear. It's getting chilly again." Lydia had followed me out and now stood holding out her sweater to me.

Trying to fake a smile, I took the sweater from her. "Thank you," I said.

"You'll have to do a lot better than that if you don't want him to know you've been crying over him."

Alarmed, I turned away from her. "I don't know what you're talking about!"

Behind me, Lydia chuckled. "Oh now, dear Pegs, these eyes may be old, but they are still very keen. I know how you feel about him. You mustn't let what happened last night tear you apart."

"How could he? And Alice of all people!"

"Darling, we're all human. Billy knows us, and he knows what we need to keep us happy. Do you think it's just a coincidence that he always asks Alistair to tea when the poor old thing is feeling down? Or it is just by chance that he buys you chips right after Alice has been hateful to you? He did what he did because sometimes Harry can be an ass and sometimes Alice needs to know she's still the prettiest girl at the fair! Besides, you can't know what actually happened any more than I do. Now, dry those tears and let's go back inside." She took my face in her hands and wiped my eyes with a lavender scented hanky.

I calmed myself down and nodded. Not that I agreed with Lydia; I certainly did not. I knew what had happened in Alice's room as sure as I knew my own name, and Billy was no longer noble or kind. He was lecherous and duplicitous, and I hated him! But I also knew I couldn't bear him knowing how I felt. So I threw my head back, squared my shoulders, and smiled.

"That's my girl." Lydia smiled approvingly at me.

"Come on, now. Time for your grand entrance."

"Oh, Lydia," I said as I walked back around to the front of the inn with her. "I'm not an actress. You are."

Wrapping her arm around my waist, she said something I'll never forget. She said, "That's where you're wrong, my love. We all are players, every single one of us. Dear William never wrote a truer thing when he wrote, 'Life's but a walking shadow, a poor player, that struts and frets his hour upon the stage, and then is heard no more.' Listen to me, dear Pegs. Listen and remember."

When we got back to the dining room, the rest of the company was there. I had lost my seat next to Billy to sweet little Alice, who was busy fussing over his tea. Harry sat across from them, looking murderous.

"Everything all right, darling?" Alistair asked Lydia.

"Just fine, dear. Pegs just had a little homesickness. Nothing to worry about."

"Oh, poor Pegs. So far from home and so lonely. Come sit by me, pet, and I'll be your shoulder to cry on." Alice's face was all concern, but I saw the look of triumph in her eyes. She and I both knew she had bested me, and she wasn't about to let me forget it.

"I'll be fine, thank you, Alice." I ended up sitting next to Harry across the table from her. He smelled of old beer and cheap perfume. From the look on his face, I could tell that Alice's attentiveness to Billy was not being well received.

"Well, now that we are all back, I have an announcement to make." Billy stood up and rapped a spoon on the table to get everyone's attention.

"Tomorrow we will arrive in…Cottswattington!"

A collective gasp rose up from the troupe.

"And…" he continued with great flourish, "we have been permitted to perform in Wildes!"

The whole room exploded into conversation! Billy sat back down and winked at me from across the table.

Alice was beside herself. "Billy, you're a miracle worker! Imagine… Wildes, after all this time. Oh, we are doing the Scottish play, aren't we? We must! We simply must!"

"Do you mean Macbeth?" I asked.

You could have heard a pin drop in that room. My simple question had rendered everyone speechless.

"Was I wrong?" I asked, embarrassed. "So you're not doing Macbeth?"

"Oh, she said it again!" Alice squealed, putting her hands over her ears.

Alistair leaned over toward me from the end of the

table, his face stern. "You must not say that, Pegs. You must not!"

I was taken aback. No one had ever barked at me the whole time I had been with them. Now they all looked at me as if I had just said a dirty word. All except Billy, who was trying to hide his laughter behind a napkin.

"Calm down, Alistair. Pegs is not familiar with our silly superstitions. She didn't mean any harm." He wiped his eyes with the cloth, still giggling.

"But you must tell her, Billy, or who knows what could happen." Even Lydia seemed afraid of me.

"Fine, I will tell her. She'll need the whole story to understand anyway. Pegs, did you ever wonder why so many of us pull on your ponytail so often?"

I nodded. This strange habit had started the first night of the very first performance. Since then, it happened so often that I barely noticed it.

"Well, the first night Mike did it to be playful," Billy said, "and if you will remember, he performed very well that night, netting two curtain calls. He thought it might have brought him good luck, so he did it again the next night. And again, the audience loved him. You see, Pegs, it has become a bit of a good luck thing for us. And we are always looking around for good luck and how to thwart bad luck."

(Let me take a moment to educate you about theater people. Theater people are some of the most superstitious people on the planet. I think it has to do with their lives being so gypsy-like, moving on from one place to the next, full of uncertainty about how the show will go from night to night. They are also much more attuned to the subtle, invisible forces that move around us, so much more in tune than, say, a stockbroker or a bricklayer. It's almost as if they were born that way.)

Billy continued with his explanation. “Now, the play that you so indiscriminately mentioned has long been associated with bad luck. Therefore, some rather interesting superstitions have grown up around it, one of them being: If you intend to perform the play, you cannot say its name, nor can you refer to the two main characters by name. They should only be referred to as Mr. and Mrs. M.” Smiling at me, he took a sip of his tea.

My practical American mind was getting a bit riled up at this point, so I pressed him for more answers. “That’s completely silly,” I protested. “Why would a play be considered bad luck anyway? And if it is, why are you all so keen to perform it?”

Alice stirred her tea slowly “You don’t know much about Shakespeare, do you dear?” she asked snidely. I gave her a look that would have frozen Hades itself.

“Alice!” Alistair’s voice barked again. “She can’t be expected to know as much as we do! Instead of chastising her, we should enlighten her. Pegs, my girl, pour yourself a nice cup of tea and let me explain.”

Most of the people around us groaned and got up to leave. The only people who remained in the dining room were Billy, Alistair, Lydia, and I. I did as I was told and poured out a hot cup of tea.

“In order to understand our feelings about the Scottish play and Cottswattington, you have to know a little about William Shakespeare himself,” Alistair told me. “You see, not too much is known about a particular period in his life. Somewhere between 1583 and 1592, when he would have been in his twenties, no one can find any mention of him anywhere. This isn’t really too unusual for the time period he lived in. Shakespeare scholars call it ‘the lost years,’ and there has been speculation that he was everything from a sailor to a tutor to a soldier."

Alistair grew more excited. "Now, on to Cottswattington! In the same time period, the tiny hamlet of Cottswattington had a very famous and well-documented resident. They called her Mistress Meg, and she was a most notorious witch!"

I must admit that Alistair did have a way with words; I was totally engaged in the story as I sipped my tea and listened.

He went on with a gleam in his eye. "There are some who believe that young William actually knew and had a lover's relationship with Mistress Meg. When he left, he used some of the actual spells he learned from her in the Scottish play, and she, enraged at his thievery, put a curse on the play and all who would perform it."

"Cue lightening and crash of thunder!" Billy laughed. He was clearly enjoying the story himself.

With a harrumph at being interrupted, Alistair continued, "There is an old, old theater house in Cottswattington supposedly built right on the site of Mistress Meg's farm, called the Wildes House, after the man who built it. It is in this theater that several strange occurrences have been witnessed. Lights go on and off by themselves. Door locked tight at night stand wide open in the morning. Footsteps and knocking are heard when no one is about, but worst of all, there have been deaths at that theater. Many, many deaths!"

"So, why do you want to play there? And why that play of all things?" By this point, I was quite exasperated at the whole affair.

Lydia, who had taken up her knitting during the story, said softly, "We do it to pay homage, dear. There are some who believe that it is not Mistress Meg who haunts the

Wildes…"

My mouth fell slightly open.

"Do you mean… Are you saying that…that…?"

Billy nodded. "Yes, indeed, dear Pegs. Many in the theater firmly believe that William Shakespeare himself haunts yon theater of old." The mischievous man winked at me after he finished his shocking statement.

Blushing at his obvious flirting, I turned back to Alistair. "But why there? Why not Stratford-upon-Avon, or the place where the Globe stood, or Holy Trinity Church where he's buried?"

"Because of the book in the pub." All three of them said it at the same time. Then they had a laugh about it.

"What book in what pub?" I practically screeched at them.

"Oh, dear!" Lydia dropped a stich in her shock. "Don't raise your voice so, Pegs. I's not very attractive." She raised a suggestive eyebrow in Billy's direction.

"Oh, it's all right, Lydia." Alistair patted his wife on her knee. "She's just excited to hear the best part. Cottswattington has but one inn—The Inn of the Dark Woods, it's called—and supposedly it's been around since the Middle Ages. Well, in the basement of the Inn is a pub, and many, many years ago the bloke that owned it wanted to replace the floor. So he digs up the existing floor, and guess what he finds?"

"A book?" I asked.

"No, a body! And then another and another until the whole place looks like a morgue! So he calls in some help, by way of archeologists and historians and the like. They give the bodies a once-over and say these people have all had their throats slit from ear to ear. Human sacrifice, they say. One of the bodies is that of a young boy, and guess what they find holding in his hands?"

"A book?" I asked.

"No! A shiny silver dagger all covered in strange symbols! The same kind of symbols they find all around the remnants of Mistress Meg's farm. See, it was her that did the sacrificing for her bloody witches' Sabbaths. Well, they take the poor souls out and give them good Christian burials, and the bloke gets his new floor. And all seems right with the world. But then, the chimney at the old inn catches fire, nearly killing the innkeeper and his family. They manage to escape, but no one can put out the fire. It burns and burns for three days straight. Well, the townsfolk don't know what to do, so they call in a local man whose family had a long history of witch hunting. He goes into the basement of the inn, and guess what he sees in the middle of the raging fire?"

Pausing to take a calming breath, I said, "Alistair, was it a book?"

"Righto! An old black book hovering above the floor in the middle of flames! Saying the Lord's Prayer, the man reaches in and pulls out the book. Amazingly, the fire disappears. The townspeople all look at the book, and it seems to be some kind of diary. Mistress Meg's diary. In it, she says that her heart has been broken by one "Will. S." She vows that though he left her in life, he would not leave her in death. She cast a spell binding him to her home forever."

The story was so tragic and romantic and frightening, I simply had to see that book. "Can I see the book when we go?"

"Well, no," said Alistair sheepishly. "It seems the book went missing years ago. No one has seen it in ages."

"But I don't understand…" The sudden end to the story

made me lose my mental footing.

"It's simple, Pegs." Billy was wiping off his mouth after finishing his eggs. "Cottswattington is a small, out of the way place, with only one claim to fame, Mistress Meg, who was probably a very good midwife and herbalist who got a bad reputation with the housewives for being too busty or too smart. Someone with a theater background comes along and invents the love story of Will and Meg. After that, it's easy to tie it all together and invent a ghost."

Lydia's needles clacked in protest. "Ghosts are not invented, Billy. They reside among us always."

"Oh, Lydia." Billy got up from the table. "Every English town has a ghost. Show me one that doesn't, and I'll show you a lazy town council! The council at Cottswattington just has a literary bent." He tossed his napkin down on the table and left the room.

Billy's apparent unbelief in the paranormal notwithstanding, we arrived in Cottswattington very early in the morning the very next day. The best way I can describe it is to say it is a town next to a sea coast, except there is no sea. It was misty and full of dark, craggy rocks. The houses were built sturdily with the impression they were imminently facing the danger of being swept away, yet there was no crash of waves to be heard, as they were far inland. I'm sure it wasn't always as dark and foggy as I remember it, but when we were there, the sun did not make an appearance even once. Yet the townspeople, instead of being standoffish or brooding, were so friendly and excited to see us, you might have thought us royalty of some kind.

Billy and Alice were quite an item at this point, with all the cast and crew buzzing about their liaison. Alice fawned over him while Harry pouted horribly. Then he began to court her again, slowly. She would act disinterested, even though I knew she wasn't. On the other hand, Billy was so busy speaking with the townsfolk and working with the cast and crew, he often acted like he didn't give a fig if Alice was around or not.

I watched him from afar. I won't be lying when I say my jealously had turned into a murderous rage! If given half the chance, I would have broken out all the windows in bus in my anger.

But again I ramble off the mark. Let me tell you about the Wildes! It was a large, roundish building—very, very old. There were two massive doors from which you entered, and then you immediately had to walk up some steep stairs to enter the back of the theater. I dare say, if I was there now, you couldn't get my arthritic knees to make the climb.

The original building was erected in the early 1600s by a man who surely must have seemed ambitious at the time; why in the world would you build a theater in the middle of nowhere in a period of time when no one around you had the time or the money to see a play? Mr. Wildes must have been the most forward-thinking art lover in all of England.

Since then, the theater had been renovated and added onto over time, but you still felt that ancient core all around you when you were in it. It was the pride and joy of Cottswattington. The townsfolk loved that building as I have never seen before or since. If you stopped moving for even a second, they viewed your pausing as an opportunity to tell you all about it—the construction of it, the location of Mistress Meg's farm in relation to it, the legend of Will, any ghostly happenings that could be attributed to it or anything at all. It became very annoying to me.

The day we entered the theater, we were accompanied by at least two dozen townsfolk including the mayor, the town council, the vicar, the headmaster of the local school, and of course, the local historian…along with their wives and any other person Cottswattington deemed important enough to be there. With much ceremony, the round little mayor escorted us, Billy in front of course, up the steep stairs until we were all gazing down at the glossy wooden stage at the bottom.

Alice was in rare form that day. She unwrapped herself from Billy's embrace and swept down the aisles to the middle of the stage with her arms extended, as if she was soaking up psychic atmosphere.

"Oh, he's here! Can't you just feel his presence all around you?" Eyes half closed, she walked around the center of the stage, breathing deeply.

"Hey!" Mike poked me in the ribs and whispered, "If 'he' is here, I bet he drops a heavy light on 'er." I giggled because I knew that was the reaction he was hoping for. I didn't want kindly Mike to know that was the event I was praying would happen!

You'll indulge me just a few moments before we get back to the story, won't you? I wish to tell you about the effect that working in a supposedly haunted building has on you. This is, of course, assuming you have never had the experience. If you have, please feel free to skip this section.

When you know someplace has the reputation of being haunted, you most often have the option of avoiding the place in question. You don't drive down the road next to the old farmhouse. You choose an alternate route on your walk in order to avoid the house where the screams are heard or the spectral lights are seen. But when you are expected to do a job there, you lose that option. You must enter that building, attempting to put aside all the grisly knowledge you possess about it so you can focus on your task, all the time wondering if the scratching noise or the faint thumps you hear behind you are indeed the work of rats, as you have been assured, or something altogether different.

That's what it was like working in the Wildes. Since all the town was so excited to see the upcoming play, there was no need for me to go out and drum up business. Instead, Billy decided to put me to work as a backstage assistant. This wasn't new. I had often filled in, lining up props or working the lights when someone was ill or otherwise engaged. But it wasn't what I wanted to do for many reasons.

In spite of the American bravado I was currently displaying, I didn't like the Wildes building. It felt wrong to me. I could never be sure if the whispers I heard were simply the result of the good acoustics of the round theater or disembodied voices straining to be heard. And there were some places backstage I simply could not stand; I mean this in the sense that I could not bear to even pass by them. Places that felt for all the world as if someone unseen was already there, waiting and watching. I noticed others avoiding the same places, but no one spoke about it.

Billy had decided to stay the rest of the week in Cottswattington because the town was putting us up for free, and he really wanted the performance of the play (we discussed earlier why I won't from now on mention the name) to be perfect for the townsfolk. It was on our second day there that Alice, according to her story, was attacked by unseen hands!

I was sitting up high in the seats, following along in the script, ready for someone to call out, "Line!" It was the scene when Mr. M and Banquo encounter the three witches. Harry was Mr. M and Mike was Banquo. Billy was walking around behind them with his arms crossed, stopping them from time to time with a correction or an idea about blocking. The mood was getting pretty tense because Harry, still jealous of Billy, was refusing to do some things and being argumentative. I could feel Billy's anger rising up.

Just as the two men were about to engage in a heated battle, blood-curdling screams rang out all around us. It was Alice! Everyone started running at once. I threw down the script and raced backstage with the rest of them. Her screams of panic were terrifying. When I joined the others, Billy and Harry were trying to calm her down from the other side of a locked door.

"It's all right, darling. We're here! Just try the knob from your side. Calm down and stop shouting so."

"What's going on?" I asked Mike.

The big man was trying so hard not to laugh; tears were rolling down his face.

"She's locked in the loo," he sputtered.

Just then, Billy forced open the door and a tear-streaked, shaking Alice collapsed into his arms.

"It was horrible! Something grabbed my hair!" A theatrically shaking hand reached up to point at her silver blonde tresses, which were indeed disheveled.

"That's impossible." Billy unceremoniously dropped her into Harry's arms and went to investigate the door.

Harry cradled her like a child. Gently he stroked her face. "Shhh. Tell us what happened, darling."

Alice gazed up at him like he was Lancelot and she was Guinevere. In a halting voice, she said, "I was standing watching you rehearse when suddenly something grabbed the top of my hair, and I was pulled backward into that dreadful dark room. I heard the door shut and the lock click. Then I knew I was locked inside with it! I began to scream and…and…you came and saved me." She reached her hand up to gently touch Harry's lips. Again, I mentally encouraged Will to drop the light.

"Nonsense," barked Billy. Rather roughly, he pulled her up to standing. "Look here, Alice. You were standing right here. See? You can see right onto the stage from here." He stood where he indicated. "See, you were right in front of the loo door, and look here!" He pointed to a nail that jutted out of the loo doorframe. The nail had several strands of white-blonde hair hanging from it.

"You caught your hair on the nail, and it pulled it. Then you stumbled backwards. See, the threshold of the loo is uneven, raised up in a way. So you stumbled backwards into the loo and knocked the door shut behind you in your panic. And look here…" He entered the loo and slammed the door.

He tried the door knob several times in vain.

"It jams, see! The wood is so old and warped, it just got stuck!" With a bang, he managed to open the door suddenly.

The rest of the cast and crew groaned at her in disgust. Even Harry rolled his eyes. Everyone wandered off back to where they had been before the shouting began. But Alice kept repeating, "No! That's not what happened! I felt hands on me, real hands!"

I started back to my perch when Alice rushed over to me. The fear in her eyes was evident.

"Pegs," she said desperately, "I felt hands on me. Something pulled me into that room!" It was the only time I felt sure she wasn't acting.

The night of the performance was very windy. The wind itself was like a living thing stalking us. Somehow you could hear it approaching before it reached you, so you braced for it. Inside the Wildes, we could hear it trying to tear the roof off.

"I hope this ancient old place is as strong as it looks tonight." Billy was putting on the rest of his makeup back stage. He was playing the part of Macduff because Leonard, another actor in the troupe, had gotten so frightened by something that he would not speak about, but that made him refuse to even enter the theater after the first day of rehearsal.

"So, do you think I can, tonight, Billy…you know…be backstage?"

Billy was being badgered by Thomas, the youngest member of our troupe. Thomas was someone's nephew, and he dearly wanted to be an actor. He worshipped Billy and Harry to the point of being silly. Just barely seventeen, he was the clumsiest boy I had ever met. He could trip and fall on a bare floor. Billy always had him up away from the stage working the lights, but he wanted to be backstage during a performance more than anything.

"Not tonight, Tom. There are just so many times the swords get switched out. I need you up there working that decrepit lighting system. You're the best at the electrical!"

Billy was trying to soften the blow to the boy. You see, we had two sets of swords for the play. One set was a real set that Billy had been given as a gift by some famous actor. This set was very special to Billy, and it was only to be used in scenes when the actor was not fighting; they were just for show. Then there were a set of prop swords that Billy had made to look just like the originals. These swords collapsed in on themselves when they were thrust against someone. It looked like they went straight through, giving the audience a gasping thrill.

The only way to tell them apart was that the real swords were marked with a small piece of red tape, while the fake ones had a small piece of blue tape. In the Scottish play, they were switched a couple of times, most importantly at the end when the big fight scene between Macduff and Mr. M takes place.

Billy was too worried the overzealous boy would get them all mixed up.

"Oh, all right." Thomas hung his head. I felt sorry for him.

I was on prop duty that night. And I wasn't looking forward to it. I had been told to stand exactly in one of those horrible places I couldn't bear and for the whole night. Dreadful! Billy walked over to me and pulled my pony tail.

"Done!" he announced. "Now I'll be sure to have a good show."

I didn't say anything to him. I just turned away, adjusting some of the items on the prop table. My heart still ached from his betrayal.

"Pegs, you've been awfully quiet around me lately. Is there anything wrong?"

He had noticed. And he cared! Here was my chance to declare my love for him, or at least to tell him what a snake I thought him to be. But my courage failed when I looked up at his worried face.

"It's nothing. I'm fine," was all I said.

"All right then." He smiled at me, satisfied that all was well. "But Pegs, if you ever need to talk to me, I'm right here, you know. I just want to tell you that Harry, well, there are lots and lots of Harrys in the world, and you will break all their hearts."

"What?" I thought to myself. Harry? He thought I was in love with Harry. He thought I was pining and moping about Harry! I actually felt my heart break apart. The pain was excruciating! Standing there pale and shaking, I watched Billy walk off. I would have cried if I'd had the strength.

"Are you sick? You look like you've just seen ol' Will himself." Thomas had walked back up to me after composing himself in the loo.

"Thomas…" I said in a far off voice. "I don't feel well. I want to switch with you. I'll work the lights tonight. You do the props." I couldn't be backstage that night at all. One more time of seeing Billy and I would burst into tears, I just knew it! I had to be alone, and up in the light booth at the way back of the theater was my only refuge.

"Really?" The boy was ecstatic. "Oh thanks, Pegs! Now, I better get all these props set just right." He busied himself rearranging things as I walked like a zombie to the light booth.

Once there, I cried until I made myself sick. I cried as I moved the spotlight around the stage. I sobbed as I set the blue and purple lights for the witches. I wept uncontrollably as I adjusted the red light for the murder of Duncan. I cried until my chest hurt.

Finally, I had a moment to sit still. Looking down, I could see Billy going on about how all his children had been murdered, and sure enough, I thought him so brilliant I cried again. There is no point trying to describe how I felt. If you have never loved someone who so completely never loved you, consider yourself very lucky indeed.

So involved was I in my own misery that I hadn't been paying attention to the play at all. Suddenly, my ponytail received a strong yank. Startled, I spun around expecting to see Mike or someone behind me. There was no one there.

I looked down on the stage. It was almost the end of the play, and the audience seemed rapt by it. Noticing the curtains fluttering on stage left, I glanced over to see a frantic looking Mike and Alistair attempting to get Harry's attention. But Harry was in the middle of a stirring soliloquy and was not paying them any attention.

Just then Billy entered from stage right. My goodness, he looked glorious! It was the final fight scene where the audience finds out that Macduff was born by medieval Caesarean section. Therefore, he was not actually born of a woman, and he is the only one who can kill the evil Mr. M. Billy was brilliant. He said his lines with such fervor and finesse. He seemed so full of life, he almost put off a glow of energy.

Harry was equally stunning. You could tell that all the rage he felt at Billy over Alice was brimming over, making the fight scene seem real. Suddenly, Harry lunged with his sword full out at Billy, just missing him. Billy parried and managed to knock the sword from Harry's hand. Then he threw his own sword away and lunged at Harry's throat with his bare hands. The two men fell to the floor in a real life or death struggle.

What was going on? I wondered. This simply wasn't how the scene was rehearsed. What in the world was Billy doing?

The audience was leaning forward in their seats, horrified yet delighted at the same time. I thought the two men were going to kill each other. Finally, Billy pulled out a gleaming silver dagger, letting it catch the light for brief moment before he plunged in into Harry's heart. I truly thought he was killed! Harry looked stunned for a moment, but then I noticed he went into his usual badly acted death throes, so I knew he was all right. Billy stood and delivered his lines of triumph at killing Mr. M, even though that event was supposed to happen offstage.

The crowd couldn't control themselves any longer. When Billy stood holding the dagger above his head and called out, "Hail, King of Scotland," they rose to their feet cheering and clapping. Someone dropped the curtain. Between the audience and the wind, the noise in the theater was thunderous.

Actors then began to come out to take their bows. Each one received the same adoration as Billy had. Alice and Harry stood hand in hand, bowing and blowing kisses. Alistair and Mike smiled and pranced about, mugging for the crowd. Finally, Billy stumbled on stage. The roar rose up again. But instead of bowing, Billy looked confused. He stood awkwardly, as though not knowing what to do. Mike, Alistair, Harry, and Alice surrounded him, congratulating him. Billy shyly thanked them and took one or two tentative bows to the crowd before groping his way off the stage.

It seemed like hours before everyone left. I was determined to stay up in that light booth until everyone had gone. At last only Billy remained. He walked up and down the stage, looking all around, lost in thought. Feeling I had to face him sometime, I bashfully came out of the booth and walked down the aisle toward the stage.

When he heard me coming, he glanced up in alarm. Once he saw me, he turned back away into his thoughts.

"There she is," a voice called. "We've been looking all over for you. Good show, girl. Damned good show!" Alistair and Lydia approached me from backstage. Lydia wrapped her arms around me.

"You have our dearest thanks, child. Dear, dear Pegs!" She looked at me lovingly.

"Were the lights really that good?" I asked, not knowing what else to say.

Mike came up from behind, picking me up in a bear hug. "Look at her joking!" he said.

"I'm not sure I know what to say," I stammered.

"If we hadn't seen you on the catwalk pointing frantically at the prop table, we never would have known," continued Alistair.

"I'm not sure what you mean," I said.

Billy was leaning up against the stage wall, with his arms crossed. Hearing my confusion, he raised his head, looking at me meaningfully. "They saw you on the catwalk gesturing frantically at the prop table. It seems that Thomas had mixed up the swords, giving Harry and me the real ones for the fight scene. Mike and Alistair tried to distract us so we wouldn't run each other through. You remember now, don't you, Pegs?" The look in his eyes was stern. The implication being I had better say I remembered.

Too stunned to speak, I just stammered, "But I wasn't…"

"And you, my boy… The performance of a lifetime!" Alistair walked over to Billy, patting him on the shoulder. "How you knocked the sword out of Harry's hand! And the death scene. What a way to improvise! That bit with the dagger was brilliant. Where did you get it, boy? It was stunning. All that bright silver…like it was giving off a light of its own!"

Laughing, Billy rubbed his neck with his hands. "Trade secrets, old man. Trade secrets."

"We better get to that party before Harry and Alice start performing again." Lydia was rushing down the stage stairs. "It seems you have been replaced, Mr. Summerfield." She shot that last comment back over her shoulder at Billy.

"And not a moment too soon," was Billy's mumbled reply.

They all left. I heard the front door slam. It was only Billy and me standing on the empty stage. I looked around, still confused. I simply could not fathom what had happened. Softly I said as much to Billy. He walked over to stand next to me.

"It seems that someone, pretending to be you, was trying to warn us that the swords had been switched, and whoever that caring person was, he wanted to save someone's life. But who it was, or what it was, I can't say we ever will really know."

"But didn't you see anyone? How did you know to knock the sword from Harry's hand?"

"Ah, well, that's just the thing. You see, just before that final scene, I saw you motioning me to come to you. You were standing backstage right by the loo door. I went over, and I must have tripped or something, because I spent the last fifteen minutes of the play locked behind the blasted loo door. I only got out just as the curtain fell. Then everyone pulled me onstage to thunderous applause, telling me I had brought the house down. Only it wasn't me."

We both looked around at the dimly lit theater. Remembering the tug on my hair in the light booth, I shuddered. Had something unseen decided to partake in our troupe's lucky tradition?

Billy and I never discussed it. I tried a few times, but he always changed the subject. It wasn't long after that I ended my employment with the Summerfield Troupe and headed home.

Now time has forced me to slow down; it simply won't allow my body to keep up anymore, but my mind has not slowed. Now is the time of remembering.

If what I think happened that night did actually happen, it makes sense to me how The Bard would have chosen the part of Billy for himself. They were so similar! Both he and Billy had a traveling group of actors. Both he and Billy loved the theater more than anything else. Both he and Billy had a reputation with the ladies. Why, they even had the same initials, as Billy's given name was William!

But why choose me? Me—a girl with no real interest in

the stage or acting, someone who only had the most marginal knowledge of his works. There is no way to ever be sure, but I do have a theory.

I think it was the love and loss I felt that night which drew him to me. The deep, painful ache of my young heart may have reached out somehow and connected with him. After that night, I began to read all he ever wrote, and I know he had known the same sadness.

I take comfort in the knowledge that it will not be long now. Soon it will all go very still and only the light, airy essence of my being will remain, but just for a moment. Then at last, the teller of stories that I am will finally become a story of my own.

Perchance to Dream

by Donna A. Leahey

I wake, the fog of sleep falling away in a moment, as it does when one is startled from slumber. I sit up, confused and nervous; the room is dim, lit only by the moon leaching away the color and painting everything silver.

I look to my left, to the window, but the sheer curtains cover it and I can see nothing outside but a splash of headlights from a car on the street below. To my right is my enormous mirror in its gilded frame. I love that mirror. I see my reflection, disheveled from tossing and turning, the white of my nightgown cutting through the darkness.

In the mirror, my reflection stares back at me; her gaze meets mine. She is as confused and startled as I. As we look at each other, the shadows behind her begin to move and a pair of bright, malevolent eyes open, looking not at her, but right at me. I scream and leap from bed, whirling about to face the intruder!

...but there is no one there.

I turn back to the mirror and am surprised to find my reflection is still sitting up in bed, regarding me with a cocked head and wide eyes. The shadow has crept closer to her. I point, screaming a warning, but my reflection only frowns at me as the shadow lifts a long-fingered, clawed hand. There is something wrong with that hand, I notice, not only does it have too many fingers, but each of the fingers has too many joints. I scream again as the shadow grabs my reflection by the hair and drags her backward off the bed. Her feet kick frantically as she vanishes from sight. There is no sound, but surely she must be screaming with fright.

"No! No!" I scream and run to the mirror. I smack my palms against the smooth surface, leaving prints on the otherwise pristine glass. The shadow raises its head above the edge of the bed and once again looks right at me with its bright eyes.

There is nothing to the shadow but darkness, an absence of light. If it has form, if it has bulk, it is hidden in the shifting and moving darkness surrounding it. From the black depths, its eyes shine at me. It smiles, and only then can I see the thin lips stretching wide and then wider across its absent face, thin lips parting to reveal teeth like a shark's, repeating endlessly back into the dark cavern of its mouth.

I step back from the mirror, my heart racing. The shadow is moving, dragging my reflection behind it, across the floor and out the door. She is still and quiet but for the movement of her chest as she breathes. A thin trail of blood is left by her dragging heels, parallel lines, slick and moist, a dark greasy gray in the colorless light.

I stare at the reflection of the room, identical in every way to the room in which I stand but for the lines of blood and my presence. I race out into the hallway, but she is not there. Of course she's not; she's my reflection and there is no mirror here.

There is, however, a large white rabbit with pink eyes. He plucks a watch from a pocket on his fine silk waistcoat and declares, "Oh dear! Oh dear! I shall be too late!" before he vanishes down a rabbit hole which I have never before noticed there in my hallway.

"I'm dreaming," I whisper, but it is more hope than conviction that makes me say it.

I hurry into the guest room where there is an antique vanity with a large oval mirror. There on the coverlet is Duke, the German Shepherd who was my dearest friend when I was ten. He's been dead for fifteen years, but still he wags his tail at me and has the grace to look embarrassed about being on the bed. He knows better.

I waste no time on Duke, though I loved him dearly. Within the mirror I see the shadow. It's as if it had paused there in the doorway to be sure I could see it. My reflection is beginning to wake, making small twitches and jerks, and her eyes are fluttering. However, the shadow pays no attention to her. It stares at me instead, its grin growing wider and wider until it seems its face must split in two. Then my reflection wakes, sitting up and opening her mouth in a wide and terrified scream, though I hear nothing. The shadow tangles its fingers in her hair once again and drags her kicking and fighting from sight. Duke gazes at me with his worried face, but then he tucks his nose under his tail and curls himself into a tighter and tighter ball until he disappears.

I hurry back out into the hall where I'm greeted by Poseidon, the god of the sea. He sits astride a dolphin who is swimming with perfect contentment above the long, darkly patterned hall runner. "It's going to kill her, you know," Poseidon says, stroking his long beard.

"And eat her liver with some fava beans and a nice Chianti," the dolphin adds.

"I'm having a dream," I say, but they swim away down the hall and vanish into my bedroom without a further response. I have no time to worry about whether the wet spot on the runner is sea water or dolphin pee; I hurry to the bathroom with its plethora of mirrors. The shadow holds my reflection down with one hand, waiting for me. When we make eye contact, it gives me a little finger wave. With all those joints on all those fingers, it is a ghastly sight, like a spindly-legged spider waving all its legs in the air.

I have no time to wonder at it, though, as it moves too fast to see and rakes its claws down my reflection's chest and belly. Blood begins to flow from the wounds, and then a horde of butterflies swarm in through the window and begin to flit about the room. Only, they're not truly butterflies; they're tarantulas with colorful butterfly wings. Only, they're not really tarantulas either, I notice, when one turns to look at me with its eight very human eyes. It flits up and down, back and forth, regarding me with great seriousness. Then it opens its mouth to reveal teeth like a tiger's before it zips over to my reflection, now completely hidden behind the colorful wings. Nine white cats slink into view as well, and crouch around the periphery, happily lapping up the spreading pool of blood.

"That can't be good for them," the Queen of Hearts offers from where she lounges in my bathtub, which is filled with bubbles and rose petals. When I look back, the cats have all turned the same color as the blood. The spiderflies lift into the air and begin to circle the room in a rainbow display of bright colors. The blood is completely gone. In fact, my reflection is completely gone. The spiderflies have her! Her fingers reach out through the mass of wings. Her feet kick faintly, seeking the floor below. The shadow cocks its head and smirks at me as the horde of spiderflies flit out the door and down the hall, burdened by my reflection. The cats march out after them in a long line, and the shadow follows, his eyes never leaving mine until he is out of sight of the mirror.

"Oh God!" I whisper. "This must be a dream. Please, let it be a dream."

From the bath behind me I hear, "We're all mad here!"

and "Why is a raven like a writing desk?" But I pay the voices no attention as I hurry from the bathroom. Twin little blonde girls stand in my way, staring at me balefully. They are holding hands and wearing matching pale blue dresses with knee socks and Mary Janes.

"Leave me alone!"

They vanish in a puff of blue smoke as I rush past them. I hurry down the stairs, my bare feet making next to no sound on the carpet. I pause near the bottom. I have mirrors in every room of my house. I've always loved them, the way they brighten a room, make it seem bigger. The shadow could be anywhere, but I think I know where I'll find it.

The staircase opens into the living room, where a rectangular mirror rests above the hearth. Several of the spiderflies flit about within that mirror, but I do not see the shadow, nor my reflection.

I pace past my office where the oval stand mirror with mahogany frame holds court, and the kitchen, where the mirror with beveled edges is mounted on the pantry door. The downstairs bathroom has a mirror on the door and above the sink. I look into none of them.

Duke appears before me, blocking the way into the dining room. "It's going to kill her, you know," he says, with a surprisingly suave English accent. He wags his tail at me, but his brown eyes are sad.

"I know," I say.

Duke swirls about and is replaced by the white rabbit. "You're late! You're late!" he squeaks urgently and vanishes into the rabbit hole at his feet.

I try to wake up. I pinch myself, even smack myself in the face. Poseidon watches me with a quizzical expression, but I can't wake myself up. I even scream out loud, "Wake up!

Wake up! Wake up now!" ...to no avail. Poseidon shrugs at me and his dolphin swims away.

I peer into the dining room and am unsurprised to see the shadow there in the mirror. The far wall of the rectangular room is entirely mirrored tile. It makes the room seem so big and bright. I've always loved it. But tonight, on this night...

The image in the mirror makes me scream into hands cupped over my mouth. The spiderflies lower my writhing reflection to the dining table. Her white nightgown is torn and stained with blood. Her thrashing legs knock the enormous candelabra to the floor. As the shadow meets my eyes and smiles, the cats trot into the room. One by one, they drape across my reflection's ankles, her wrists... One lies on her hips, her belly, her chest.

Once again, her eyes find mine, and I see her lips forming words I can't make out. But then one of the cats curls up in her hair, and the ninth cat flops down over her eyes. She is held helpless by them, unable to move. The shadow, never taking its eyes from me, circles the table, ignoring my reflection's screams and struggles. She's so very frightened, but I can't help her.

The shadow's long-fingered hands hover over my reflection's body, wiggling like spider legs. With exaggerated gentleness it lifts her gown and splits it from hem to neck, laying it open so her body is exposed. With one claw extended it traces a line, a line that fills with blood, along the base of her rib cage on the right side of her body. Right over her liver.

Its shining eyes glint at me; it knows it's won. One spidery hand trails across my reflection's skin while wiggling the fingers of the other hand at me in another mocking finger wave. Its triumph is complete.

I shake my head. No. I know I'm dreaming. It's my dream and I will take control. I know how to beat it, how to kill it. It lives inside the mirror.

"NO!" I scream. I dart forward, snatch the candelabra from where it rests on the floor, and charge at the mirror. The shadow lifts its hands to guard its face. The cats scatter away from my reflection.

"NO! NO! NO!" I smash the candelabra into the glass. The mirror shatters with a deafening crash, but the shadow shatters as well. He falls into pieces on the carpet below. My reflection sits up. Tears run down her face and she points towards me. Her lips move...

...I wake, the fog of sleep falling away in a moment, as it does when one is startled awake. I sit up, confused and nervous; the room is dim, lit only by the moon leaching away the color and painting everything silver.

I look to the left, to the window, and then to the enormous mirror to my right. I love that mirror, though I am startled to notice it is marred by a pair of hand prints. I see my reflection, disheveled from tossing and turning, the white of my nightgown cutting through the darkness. Her eyes flick behind me suddenly and she leaps from the bed, her head casting about before she looks back at me, pointing, her mouth opening in a scream!

...Then I feel the long fingers tangling into my hair.

The Three Little Pigs and the Big Bad Farmer

by L.A. Smith

Once upon a time, there were three little pigs, Moe, Larry and Curly. They lived on a farm in a nice, big, comfortable pen (by piggy standards) and were very happy. Well, mostly happy. Things hadn't been the same lately. The piggies hadn't seen Farmer Brown since he came back from town several days ago. They had not eaten since then and had run out of water yesterday. The poor little piggies were almost at their wit's end, when finally they saw Farmer Brown walking down to the barnyard...

"Hey Moe, Curly! Farmer Brown's coming!" yelled Larry.

Moe and Curly jumped up from the now dry mud hole where they were reminiscing about wonderful mud baths of the past and rushed over to where Larry stood, snout pressed through the slats of the fence.

"Yay! Suppertime!" said Curly.

"It's about freaking time he got his ass out here," Moe said. "We haven't eaten for days!"

The three of them stood there waiting expectantly as Farmer Brown drew closer. He was walking very slowly and seemed a bit awkward on his feet.

Larry snorted. "Looks like something is wrong with Farmer Brown."

"Maybe he's not feeling well," Moe said. "That might be why we haven't seen him lately."

"I hope he brings food," Curly whined. "I'm starving."

All three pigs were staring at Farmer Brown, stomachs growling, mouths parched, willing him to hurry. So all three pigs were watching when Farmer Brown stopped, snatched up a chicken that walked across his path, and proceeded to rip its head off and start chowing down on the hapless bird.

"AHHHH!" The three little pigs yelled in unison.

"Oh my God! What's wrong with Farmer Brown?" Larry said.

"Maybe he's just really hungry...like us?" Curly asked.

Moe looked at Curly like he was stupid, which he was. "Shut up, dumbass. Have you ever seen Farmer Brown eat a chicken like that before?"

They all looked back at Farmer Brown, who was now done with his chicken snack and looking around for more. Finding no more chickens stupid enough to still be within his reach, Farmer Brown looked up and spotted the horses in the pen next to the pigs. He stumbled towards them.

"Oh my God! He's going for the horses now!" Larry

said.

"They're big. One of those should fill him up," Curly added. "I hope when he's done eating, he comes and feeds us. I'm pretty thirsty too."

Moe snorted, ignored Curly, and said to Larry, "There is something seriously wrong with Farmer Brown."

"There sure is, if he thinks he's gonna catch one of those horses after they saw what he did to that chicken," Larry said.

Sure enough, the horses were going crazy, snorting and stamping their feet. As Farmer Brown got closer, they started running around in their small pen, looking for an escape. The famished Farmer reached the gate and fumbled around with it for a minute until he got lucky. The gate opened wide and he stumbled onward. He didn't have much luck in catching a horse though, and only managed to stir them into a frenzy.

The pigs, now cowering at the far side of their pen, as far away from the ruckus as possible, looked on in fascinated horror as Farmer Brown lurched around the horse pen, arms wide, trying to catch his next meal. Crazy with fear, the horses were running back and forth in their enclosure, bouncing off each other in their search for an escape. A few of them found it through the gate Farmer Brown left open. One of the horses, cornered by the crazed man, backed into the fence separating the horse pen from the pig pen and crashed through. The sharp, broken edges of a board pierced the horse's flank, and the pain spurred him forward. He ran toward Farmer Brown, reared up, knocked the grasping, grunting psycho to the ground and trampled over the man while escaping.

The pigs huddled together, shocked at what they had just witnessed. All the horses were gone and Farmer Brown lay flopping around in the dirt, struggling to get up. Curly broke the silence.

"Should we go try and help him up? Maybe he'll feed us. I'm really hungry and thirsty."

Moe and Larry looked at Curly like he was an idiot, which he was.

"Shut up about your stomach! He's not going to feed us, you moron," Moe said. "He's going to eat us."

"If he catches us," Larry added.

"You're right, we gotta run, guys," Moe said, "Before Farmer Brown gets up. Come on!"

Curly squealed, "You mean leave the pen? We can't. This is our home. I like it here."

"Curly!" Moe yelled, "Farmer Fucking Brown is gonna eat your ass if you stay here. You gotta come with us."

"No, I can't. I'm afraid," Curly said, shaking his head and backing up. "I'll hide in the haystack. He won't find me there. I'll be okay." And with that, Curly turned, ran headfirst into the big pile of hay heaped up in the corner of their pen, and disappeared from view. Except for his quivering, curly tail.

"What a dumbass!" Larry said.

"Come on," Moe said. "We can't worry about him. We gotta get out of here. Maybe he'll get lucky."

Larry snorted. "Maybe he'll keep Farmer Brown busy while we escape."

"Harsh, bro."

"Just sayin'."

"Come on! Let's get the hell out of here."

The two little pigs ran through the break in the fence. As they passed Farmer Brown, they were shocked by the sight of their beloved caretaker wallowing and struggling on the ground. The hooves of the escaping horse had done a number on him. There were a couple of dusty horseshoe prints on his body, but one hoof had managed to puncture the fallen farmer's stomach. His snake-like intestines were wriggling free as the man rolled around, trying to get up. Both pigs steered clear of Farmer Brown's grasping arms and ran for the open gate. They were free!

Having never been outside of the pen before, they didn't know which way to go, so they followed the horses into the cow pasture. They hadn't gone far when they heard a loud squeal. Stopping abruptly, they turned back to look. There was nothing to see, but they heard a cacophony of squealing. Then suddenly, all was quiet.

"I guess Curly's hiding spot didn't work out too well for him," Larry said.

"Well, I didn't think it would. But what can you do? He's an idiot."

"Was an idiot."

"Whatever."

They both stood there in a moment of silent contemplation. Larry spoke first. "So...did you take a look at Farmer Brown back there?"

Moe looked incredulously at Larry. "Yeah. I saw him."

"So...how about explaining that shit to me, because I don't get it. First, Farmer Brown starts trying to eat everything he can catch, and then that horse plows into him, punches holes in him, his guts all spilling out, and he's still kicking, trying to get up. That is just NOT freaking normal."

"I don't know, dude. You're right about it not being normal. Something is definitely wrong," Moe paused. "Did you smell him when we ran past? He smelled...dead. And like he'd been dead for a while too."

"Yeah, I smelled him...like leftover slop with a week-old drowned rat in it...on a hot day. God, that makes me hungry."

Moe nodded. "Okay, let's get going before we have company."

It didn't take long for Moe and Larry to reach the fence at the edge of the cow pasture.

"What now?" Larry asked.

Moe checked both directions. The fence looked as if it went on forever each way. He made a choice. "Let's go right."

The two pigs followed the fence-line, one in front of the other until it led them...right back to the farmyard! They stood at the side of the driveway that led up to the house. The gate that led to the world outside...to freedom...was shut tight.

Both pigs stood there, hungry and weary, not knowing what to do.

"Maybe we should have gone the other way," Larry said.

Moe looked at him like he was their recently deceased brother. "Good one, dumbass. Then we'd be standing on THAT side of the road instead of this one. Shut up before I start calling you Curly."

"You don't have to be such an ass. I'm tired and hungry and thirsty. It's no wonder I'm not thinking straight."

"I know, bro. We can at least get something to drink. Farmer Brown keeps a big tub of water out for Rex. There's sure to be some left."

"You mean we gotta go back up there?" Larry asked.

"Well, do you have any other suggestions?"

Larry didn't say anything.

"I didn't think so. Come on, keep your eyes open and squeal if you see anything."

The two pigs slowly made their way back to the farmhouse, keeping a furtive eye out for Farmer Brown. He was nowhere to be seen, so they made their way to the back of the house where Rex's food and water containers were kept. All was quiet...too quiet.

"Where's Rex? Now that I think of it, I haven't seen him around for a while," Larry said.

"If I had to take a guess, I'd say he was probably Farmer Brown's appetizer."

"Bro, I bet you're right." Larry paused a moment. "Couldn't have happened to a better dog. I hated that butt-sniffing, leg-humping, all-night-long-barking piece of fur."

"Shut up!" Moe snapped. "You wanna join him?"

Larry looked contrite and kept his mouth shut.

After a few moments, Moe whispered, "I think the coast is clear. Let's go get a drink."

The two pigs crept up to the water tub. Sure enough, Moe had been right. It was half full, plenty of water for the two of them. They drank greedily from the tub. They were so busy slurping and gulping that they almost didn't hear danger coming until it was too late.

Just in the nick of time, Moe heard grunting and groaning and looked up to see the psycho sicko farmer coming at them with hands outstretched and mouth open wide.

Squealing, Moe took off. Larry was right behind him. Turning around the corner of the house, Moe almost crashed into a huge pile of split logs. He narrowly avoided it. Larry was not so fortunate.

The unlucky pig tripped on a piece of wood and fell, causing an avalanche of split logs to tumble down upon him. Trapped, he squealed in pain and fear.

"Moe! Wait! Help me!"

Moe stopped and turned around. He started to run back but only took a few steps before he was stopped in his tracks by the horrific figure that was once his beloved Farmer Brown. The bloody, stinking mess staggered around the corner of the house, ropey intestines hanging down and trailing in the dirt. The ravenous undead figure lurched towards the fallen pig.

Larry squealed and struggled uselessly. "MOE!"

Moe backed away. "I'm sorry, bro."

"MOE!"

Moe stood paralyzed by shock as Farmer Brown threw himself on the trapped pig and took a big bite out of Larry's side. Squealing and thrashing about, Larry struggled in vain. Piece after piece, his flesh was ripped away, chewed and swallowed by the lunatic farmer, who was gorging himself on bloody mouthfuls of meat. Larry's struggles quickly diminished and then ceased altogether. The crazy, flesh-eating maniac now enjoyed his pork dinner unimpeded.

Moe, still rooted to the spot, gazed in horror at what had become of his brother. A small sound of grief escaped him.

Hearing the noise, Farmer Brown looked and saw Moe. For a moment, it seemed as if the maniacal meat-eater might be up for another chase, but the feast in front of him was too tempting. He dug his fingers into his meal once more, Moe temporarily ignored.

Finding his legs, Moe turned and ran, not paying any attention to where he was going. Looking for a place to hide, he ran helter-skelter around the farmyard, rejecting spot after spot until he spied a small, sturdy-looking brick building. He bolted for it, and upon reaching it, pushed the door in. The strong smell of stale smoke and...something else, something familiar...set him on edge.

He halted. It was dark inside. No windows. The light from the open door glinted on something hanging from the ceiling. Several somethings. Curious, the pig took a tentative step. Nothing happened, so he took another. His snout burned from the smell, so he took a breath and held it. As his eyes adjusted to the darkness, the glinting objects revealed themselves to be...hooks! Several large, pointy meat hooks hung from the ceiling. Not all of them gleamed. There were many more that didn't. They were dirty, covered in... He took another sniff... Dried blood and bits of desiccated pig flesh! He recoiled in horror.

Oh, Farmer Brown, how could you!

Moe squealed and ran out of the horrifying torture chamber. The reality that waited outside, though, was even more terrifying. Lurching toward him, merely a few paces away, was Farmer Brown! Moe squealed again and ran back inside the hellish smokehouse. He threw himself at the door and slammed it shut, but not before Butcher Brown reached a hand inside. Moe pushed as hard as he could, but the grasping hand at the end of the rotting arm would not withdraw and allow the door to close completely.

Frantic, Moe knew he couldn't hold the monster at the

door back forever. He was tired and hungry. His strength was waning. Drastic measures were called for. Mustering his courage, Moe reached out...and bit the hand that fed him! A finger was severed. It lay motionless in Moe's mouth, resting on his tongue. His first impulse was to spit it out, but something strange happened. The finger... It tasted...good. In fact, it was delicious!

Moe gave the finger a tentative chew. His eyes opened wide as the most magnificent flavor he'd ever experienced exploded inside his mouth. Munching and crunching, Moe finished eating the finger in seconds. The little pig then turned his gaze once more upon the grasping hand caught by the door.

One by one, the delicious fingers were consumed. Next, the hand. Eventually, Moe faced a dilemma. Should he let up on the door a bit and see if more of the gourmet gangrenous arm would be pushed inside? Farmer Brown had now lost a hand and part of his arm. What if he tried to escape? Maybe he didn't mind. It didn't deter him when the horse punctured his stomach and his guts fell out. Mmm...guts. Moe wondered what those tasted like.

He decided to risk it. Slowly letting his weight off the door, Moe waited breathlessly to see what would happen. Damn, the arm was removed! Moe contemplated chasing Farmer Brown down when another hand reached through the door and grabbed his snout! Moe slammed his body against the door again, trapping this hand like he had the last.

Moe smiled and snapped off a finger.

"I never knew just how much I loved Farmer Brown...until now."

About the authors:

M.A. Chiappetta officially began her writing career in the eighth grade with a riveting tale of two robots who fall in love against society's conventions. Published today, "Robots in Love" would no doubt be a blockbuster, if only a copy of it still existed. Today, she continues her quest to become famous and well-paid through copywriting, ghostwriting, teaching college-level writing, editing, and writing blogs, articles, and books of her own. She has had articles and book reviews published in *Blue Shift*, *Science Fiction and Fantasy Writer's Chat*, and *Mensa Bulletin*.

Her musings on writing, creativity, and life in general—colored by her eclectic interests in writing, music, SFF, laughter, God, and geekdom—can be found on her blog, The Chipper Muse as well as on the blog for Purple Ink Writers. You can also find her on Twitter as @chippermuse.

As a child in school, **Donna A. Leahey** turned her vocabulary homework into short stories. Years later, she is still crafting stories. Her horror short story *The Wisteria* can be found in the Eco-Horror anthology Growing Concerns. Writer, gamer, flake, Sooner, mom, dog-lover, nerd, geek, procrastinator, coffee addict, green-eyed curly girl Donna is a practicing veterinarian. She is the mother of one grown son and shares her thoughts on writing on the Purple Ink Writers blog.

Margaret Perdue is a working mother of two boys. She is a proud member of the sandwich generation, as her small household includes her aging mother and her father.

Margaret is also active in several volunteer organizations, such as PTSAs and various community organizations.

In her spare time, she trolls used bookstores for out of print, dusty, and generally quirky gothic/romance fiction. She can also be found writing in the early morning hours—books and novels for the escape artist in every woman—and on the blog for Purple Ink Writers.

She lives in Tulsa with her endlessly patient and supportive husband, two badly behaved dogs, one egotistical cat, and one violent turtle.

L.A. Smith describes herself this way:

"I write, therefore I am:

A thinker, a traveler of space and time, a hero, a villain, a romantic, a cynic, life and death, a friend, an enemy, a criminal, a victim, hope, regret, a tragedy, a happy ending, a creator, a destroyer, a monster, tears and laughter, a psychiatrist, a crazy person, a student, a teacher, a lover, a fighter, a magician, a dreamer…and so much more.

I am, therefore I write."

Purple Ink

Purple Ink is a group of writers who love the myriad, magical worlds of science fiction, fantasy, horror, weird fiction, the supernatural, alternate history…the genres collectively known as speculative fiction. We tell tall tales of ghosts, vampires, aliens, demons, and all sorts of unnatural creatures—and we have fun doing it. Oh, and we drink sometimes too. But never so much that we can't write!

Find us on Goodreads

Follow us on Facebook

Rate this book

Made in the USA
San Bernardino, CA
21 October 2015